RESOLUTION

RESOLUTION

THE RED CLAY DESERT-4

Joe Allen

iUniverse, Inc.

New York   Bloomington

Resolution
The Red Clay Desert-4

This is a work of fiction. All of the characters, names, incidents,
organizations, and dialogue in this novel are either the products
of the author's imagination or are used fictitiously.

iUniverse books may be ordered through booksellers or by contacting:

iUniverse
1663 Liberty Drive
Bloomington, IN 47403
www.iuniverse.com
1-800-Authors (1-800-288-4677)

ISBN: 978-1-4502-6241-5 (sc)
ISBN: 978-1-4502-6242-2 (ebook)

Printed in the United States of America

iUniverse rev. date: 11/03/2010

INTRODUCTION

SURVIVING THE 25th CENTURY MAY BE OUR
GREATEST CHALLENGE.

On a national scale war-like conduct, in the 25th century, continues to flourish where ideologies clash or where territorial ownership is being challenged. Additional contributions to the human riddle include mistrust of most things scientific and technological, a tendency to react without thought, and dissatisfaction with one's opportunities.

On a local scale residents are forced to trade for scarce resources, they continue to be suspicious of strangers, and religion, as always, is the provider of comfort to anxious people.

On a smaller scale even the dyed-in-the-wool loner knows his chances of survival improve if he is part of something greater than himself. Still, protection is personal and reliance on guns and knives remains.

THE MEETING

On their way to the West Coast young Blacktowers are forced to drive the broken roads of the Red Clay Desert. Heat compels them to drive at night, and darkness hinders their progress. Matt is at the steering wheel of the cumbersome old steam-powered truck built by his father, and Sweet Brady Chastain is their desert guide.

Matt is in a rush. A contingent of Chinese mercenaries want Rona Ti returned, and after his escape from jail in Nash City, he is most likely being chased by jail keepers. In an attempt to keep Matt from driving into the ditch Jane, Bobby and Rona Ti take turns walking a few yards in front of the truck.

During a rest stop the travelers from the truck are overpowered, bound, and delivered to a place of torture by desert bandits, but are they in greater danger from Pete Haze.

RESOLUTION

The Red Clay Desert-4
Joe Allen

Rona Ti made no noise as she endured her misery. Her mouth had been tied shut. Jane could see that the young Chinese girl was being violated by five pairs of persistent hands vigorously squeezing and prodding her.

Where is the man with those eyes? Jane thought.

When Jane could stand no more she screamed at the top of her voice. In the desert darkness Jane's violent outcry was so startling that three desert men jumped to their feet pulling large knives from hiding places in raggedy desert garb.

Jane heard a popping sound, and two of the men slumped to the ground. The escape of the other men was almost a cartoon-like reflex. She saw three bandits in an immediate simultaneous crouching sprint toward the protection of darkness at the edge of the firelight circle. The popping sound came once more, and two of the runners dropped face down on the clay. One runner continued, then two, then none.

Jane watched Bobbie and Matt struggling to their feet. Like her, their feet had been released, but their hands were still tied behind them. Matt led the way out of the little hollow where the festivities were being held. The ground that they ran on was hard and flat, and before long Matt found himself following the smell of smoke.

Matt had barely enough light to make out the highway as they stumbled over the curbing. The smoke was drifting in from the right so he changed course and followed the smell. In a matter of minutes Matt saw the outline of their truck. The smoke he had been following came from the dying embers of his own fire. Even though it seemed longer, Matt guessed that they had been gone less than two hours. His plan had been to use a rest stop to get beyond the blackest part of the night and allow walkers to return to the truck. The slow pace caused the truck to use too much wood and water.

When asked, none could remember their capture. Jane assumed that they had been knocked unconscious as they sat around the fire. Each person had a bump on the back of the head and they all complained about headaches.

At first glance the truck appeared to be unscathed. Matt was elated. Apparently, their captors wanted to have sport with their prisoners before ransacking the truck.

Jane started back to inspect the horses, and she jumped in surprise as a man in black stepped off the back bumper.

How could he be here ahead of us? Jane thought.

He pointed at the back of the truck as he spoke in a strangely quiet voice.

"Get in," he ordered.

"Where is Rona Ti?" Jane asked.

He nodded toward the truck box.

"I don't know who you are," Matt said, "but if you have fighting to do I'm with you. I should've been protecting us not you."

The stranger gave Matt a hard look and then ignored his remarks as he tied their feet.

"Stay in the truck," the stranger said. "I need a long rope?"

The Blacktowers watched from the back of the truck as the stranger raised the back curtain on the animal trailer, and removed Chastain's horse. The sounds of a running horse gradually faded and eventually the sound was gone.

"Rona Ti, are you okay?" Jane asked.

"Yes," Rona Ti answered, quietly

"How did he get you here so fast?" Matt asked.

"You gone, dark man make hand on mouth, say-no cry, say-no hurt, say-cover self. This one strong, carry Rona Ti-run fast."

"Could you see what they did to Chastain?" Bobbie asked.

Rona Ti looked down.

"Cut open!"

Jane shuddered at the thought.

"Bobbie and Matt, are the two of you okay?"

"I think so," Matt said. "I'll be better after the headache goes. From what I could see at their fire, we were very lucky to have Chastain as a guide. As soon as they recognized him they forgot about us. Bobbie how is your head?"

"Like everyone else," Bobbie said. "I have a bump on the back of my head, but I'm feeling better now. Getting up and around did me some good."

"One of you see if you can cut the ropes on my wrists," Matt said. "I think we have time to get fired up before he gets back, and once we get rolling we can outrun him."

"There is a butcher knife in the cabinet behind me," Jane said.

Moments later Matt was free of his bonds. After cutting Jane loose he jumped out of the back of the truck and stoked up the flames in the truck's firebox, and in no time the boiler was putting out steam. Bobbie helped feed wood into the firebox while Matt shook the grill and pumped air into the flames.

Dim light in the east allowed Matt to see an outline of the road well ahead of the truck. Little by little they picked up speed. In a matter of minutes Matt was going faster than he had ever gone, and he was starting to feel safe.

Without warning Matt and his truck roared past the man in black standing by the side of the road holding his horse. It bothered Matt that he made no effort to stop them.

As they started down hill toward a dry lakebed, Matt noticed a pair of bridges in front of him. The eastbound and westbound bridges were separate structures. Unfortunately the bridge on his side didn't go all the way across. Although Matt had plenty of room to stop he had to unhook, turn around, and return to the top of the hill in order to cross over to the other side of the highway.

The man in black stood in the path used to cross over

to the south lane. Matt didn't have to be told to stop when they reached the top of the hill. After the stranger put the horse in the trailer, he saw to it that ropes had been replaced around Blacktower ankles. The ropes were tied so they could walk but the travelers had no doubt that they were tied.

The man in black climbed into the back of the truck with Jane and Rona Ti, and he tapped on the window that connected the cab and the truck box. Bobbie opened the window.

"Stay on the south side," the dark man said. "Watch out for big cracks that be crumblin'. We be coverin' up in five or six hours. I know a place."

Quietly and deliberately the man in black checked the load in his strange looking gun and propped it against the back wall. He withdrew a long, heavy knife and it's sheath from between his shoulder blades, and placed it beside his gun. He unbuckled his equipment belt, and stacked it neatly beside the gun. He pulled off his black headscarf releasing a thick mass of long, black hair, and a beard almost as dense as the one owned by Brushy Wilkes. Next he lifted the black tunic over his head being careful not to spill any of its contents.

Jane could see that his fingers were shaking as he unlaced his moccasin-boots and kicked them into the corner. He stepped out of his trousers, and stacked these on his tunic. He pulled off his undershirt, and he looked at Jane.

"How be the China girl?"

"I think she had worse treatment from her own people."

"You got water back here?"

His voice was shaky and it hung there heavy with embarrassment. Jane could hear a hint of urgency in the asking as she handed him a cup and pointed.

"Turn the spigot on the side of my cooking water can. Take what you need, we have plenty."

The young stranger reached into the pile of clothing and took out a silver flask and unscrewed the top. The flask was filled and returned to its hiding place. Jane started to ask a question but he put a finger to his lips as he refilled the cup with water. Every movement was deliberate and exact.

The first sip of water was swished around in his mouth. His intent was to let Jane see him savoring every drop.

"Your water be good and clear, and you be generous to share with one less fortunate. Where be your water from?"

It was a formal compliment mechanically submitted by one about to consume something that belonged to another person.

"We got it from a well on the other side of Chaffee," Jane said. "Chastain, the man that got killed, showed us where to find it."

The stranger drained his cup very slowly, and he watched Jane closely as he refilled it four more times. He sipped at the fifth cupful while he asked questions.

"Who be you, and why be you here?"

Jane spared the details as she related their story to the stranger.

"Who are you?" Jane asked.

He stared at her across the top of the cup.

"My insides be too hot. You got enough water to splash a little on my outside?"

His manner changed, and he lowered his eyes when he asked for more water. Jane noticed this difference.

"What would you do if I said no you've had enough?"

"I'd be usin' what's left in the cup, unless you objected," said the stranger. "It be your water and I can't change that."

"I have questions," Jane said.

His stare hardened.

"I don't answer to women. What about the water?"

The stranger looked to the side and he was blinking. He had to steady himself by leaning forward and resting one hand on the floor. He started to tremble.

Jane saw that it bothered him considerably to ask for the water, and he asked twice. Jane took two wash pans from a cupboard and ran water into both. She placed a wedge of soap into the first pan and handed it to the man. She watched and was amazed at the care he took in washing without spilling any, and the truck was moving all the while.

He washed his hair, and he stepped out of his short pants as Jane and Rona Ti turned around. He hardly noticed. Jane pulled a clean rag from a shelf and held it until he had finished washing.

"Where do you save your used water?" he asked.

Jane took the pan of soapy water and poured what was left into a small wooden cask by the back door.

"Are you going to use the other pan of water?" she asked.

He pulled on his short pants before he answered.

"Yes, my temperature still be too high," his voice was shaky. "The only way to bring it down be splashin' on water and movin' the air."

"Stretch out face down on the floor," Jane ordered. "I wish you had told me that you were in trouble."

Jane sponged on the water and Rona Ti fanned him with one of Matt's shirts.

Jane had been so engrossed with the man's demeanor that she had ignored his appearance. Now, with him stretched out in front of her she could see that he was built a lot like Matt. He was shorter and not as heavy, but muscle stood out all over his body, he looked very solid. Like Matt, he had probably worked all his life.

How many years could that have been? Jane thought.

Jane asked him to roll over and she put her hand on his stomach. He flinched. He was still hot to the touch. It took almost an hour before she felt that he was responding, and his temperature was on the way down. He was obviously feeling better.

"I'm gonna tell you things," he said. "Not because you asked but because you deserve to know. My name be Haze, and it be five Drummonds that took you folks. They hit my place a few days ago. I picked up a hot trail comin' out of Chastain territory three days back. Yesterday, tryin' to get ahead of 'em, I got caught out in the sun. I dug in and covered up, but I got sun sick and they broke camp runnin'.

"Me and them both heard your truck a long way off and they stopped to talk and I be near to droppin'. Weren't for you and your truck I wouldn't of made it. When they saw what be making the noise, I knew I be gettin' some of them.

"I didn't know if I should help you or get the Drummonds . . . couldn't get there fast enough to keep you from getting thumped, but they be carrying you off so they weren't going far, besides I wanted to see your truck. And, when they discovered Sweet Brady Chastain, I figured they'd work on him first because they just got whipped by the Chastains. I guess you know'd you had a Chastain with you?"

"Yes," Jane said. "He was taking us as far as Tinker Prison. He told us that we could make it on our own once we were past it."

"Eventually he'd be givin' you to his people. The Chastains be the biggest bunch of killers around these parts. McSpadens and the Drummonds be next. They all got killed off once, but it looks like they be comin' back."

Haze rolled over and was quiet for a minute or two.

"I remember the Barkers, Chisholms, and Wilkes. They be clans during my granddad's time. Ain't none of the Haze Clan left but me.

"I'm going to sleep for a few minutes. Don't untie your ropes."

The interior of the truck warmed as the sun got higher in the sky. Matt could tell that midday was maybe an hour off because his shirt was soaked with sweat. Jane leaned into the cab through the window.

"Is it getting hot up here?"

"Yes, you'd better wake up your Mister Haze. I think we need to find this cover he knows about."

"Did you hear what he told us before he went to sleep?"

"We heard most of it," Bobbie answered. "It's kind of hard to hear the way he talks. Are we going to be able to get a meal ready after we stop? Ask him if we can take the ropes off while we do our work."

Haze got up from the floor and stretched.

"Keep the ropes on your ankles. If we be captured and my ropes be on you, you belong to me if I'm alive. Clans won't do nothin' to you until they settle with me."

"Then we belonged to the Drummonds last night when you freed us?" Matt asked.

"I settled with them first. Turn around at the next flat place, we have to go back a few minutes."

Haze guided Matt down a side road that led to a large concrete warehouse by the remains of an old railroad station. The doors were missing from the warehouse and Matt drove to a central position inside. He felt a noticeable drop in the temperature as soon as he entered the building.

"Will I be permitted to eat some of your food," Haze asked, looking at Matt.

"We have food and water enough for your needs," Jane answered. "It's not necessary to ask after what you did for us."

"Food and water be survival things," Haze said to Matt, "and one ain't obligated to share if there ain't enough for the one that owns 'em. It must be different where you be from."

Jane answered once more.

"Matt and I come from a big family because our men didn't have any of the afflictions that some of the young men had. Our women had to stretch the food so everybody got fed and still we never turned away a hungry person."

Haze looked at Matt.

"Do woman always do your talking?"

"They talk when they have something to say," Matt replied, without any emotion in his voice.

Haze looked at Jane out of the corner of his eyes.

"Where I trade, women folks usually hide while I be there. How good be the water in your big tank?"

"Same water as in the back," Matt replied.

"Why don't you use it to fill up your drinking water," Haze suggested, "and I'll bring you some tainted water to run your steam engine. I know of a spring on the back of the hill and it empties to a cistern. It tastes bad but it should work in your boiler."

"What about wood?" Matt asked.

"Will it burn coal?"

"Yes," Matt answered, although he didn't actually know.

"Look behind the wall over on the east side," Haze said. "Used to be half-a-load of coal behind that wall, and you can take what you need. Haze territory ain't that far away. We'll be okay once we be home."

Matt made the truck ready to go before they ate. The water tank was filled, coal was loaded, and the horses were fed and watered. After everything else was done it was time to eat and sleep.

After resuming the trip the travelers said little until the sun was low in the western sky. Suddenly Haze pointed through the front window, "That be my home," he said. It was the most Pete had said all afternoon.

They were well past Tinker Prison when Haze had Matt pull off the highway and follow a side road to an overpass.

"Use this place for midday cover," Haze said. "This road be takin' you to a river bottom with a little ground water and some shade grass and reeds for your horses. Wild cattle might graze there so it be good grass. Watch out for the bulls.

"Leave stinkin' water alone. You might run into cholera or typhoid. If you need truck water, find a level place by the river bed and dig down about four feet. Water will seep in. You might want to filter and boil whatever water you be takin' with you."

The next part was more difficult for Haze to say.

"Matt, don't be stayin' here long. And, from now on you can't even trust me. I covet your women, particularly your sister, and we would eventually fight over her. I would kill you and I wouldn't be proud of that.

"As it stands now, I helped you, you helped me. I say we be even. Agreed?"

"Agreed," Matt answered. "How long do we have?"

"I place no limits on you because you placed none on me. Take whatever you need and when you go, stay in the right side lane. I gotta sleep and that will take about ten hours. Beyond that I ain't sayin'."

Haze turned away and walked slowly up the embankment. At the top he turned.

"You can take off the ropes."

Chapter 2

It was early in the evening and Haze had just gone when Matt spoke.

"Let's get started for the river bed. If I have to dig to find water I need to get at it. Jane and Bobbie, you can make wheat flour and bake bread, and Rona Ti, you can take the horses out to graze."

Jane was feeding wood into the firebox when it occurred to her to ask a question.

"What were you and Haze talking about when you both turned and looked at me?"

Matt smiled.

"He told me that he coveted my women, particularly my sister, and, he as much as said he would fight for you if we stayed too long."

"He thinks he can just claim me?" Jane asked.

"I don't think he has a woman," Matt said, "and his chances of getting one in a place like this are poor. If he ever comes to the conclusion that this is his one and only chance for a healthy woman as pretty as you, he may decide to take you even if it means a fight. And, I think he takes his fighting very seriously. I'm not sure why he told me this, but I think there is a strange kind of honor that this kid follows."

"Do men really think I'm pretty," Jane asked, "or were you just saying that because I'm your sister?"

"You know you're pretty," Matt teased, "I saw how you looked at yourself in your mother's big mirror."

"That was a long time ago. I was just a child," Jane said seriously, "I want to know about now."

Matt thought a second.

"All I can tell you is what I heard other men say and I didn't like most of what I heard."

"You were just looking for a fight," Jane said.

"That might be," Matt admitted, "but none of my sisters ever had reason to cry about being mistreated by a man, and I didn't have to be there looking over their shoulders."

"Why do you call Haze a kid?"

"I don't think he is as old as you are. He acts like a kid."

"What about that beard?" Jane asked.

"His beard," Matt said, "is what a beard would look like if a kid never shaved. The tip ends are small, blond, and kind of worn looking. He's probably hiding bad skin or pock marks."

"Maybe he's ugly."

"Whatever it is with him," Matt warned, "don't take any chances if he comes back. Guard your mouth."

"Yeah, I remember," Jane said absentmindedly. "No questions, no answers, be seen not heard."

Matt found the riverbed with a minimum of trouble

and they proceeded with their specific tasks. Matt selected a likely place to dig for water and Bobbie started a fire a few yards away. The firelight could be seen only from the west where Rona Ti had taken the horses.

Jane ground flour, mixed bread dough, and while it was rising she carried the grill and oven down to the fire. Jane felt good about being past the dangerous part of the Red Clay Desert, so she put all of her effort and thought into her work.

It was dark when Matt hit water. The water was neither oily nor musty but it had a hint of saltiness after the filtering and boiling was finished. Matt made ready enough clean water to fill the truck's water tank and while it cooled he drained and cleaned the truck's top tank.

By first light, Matt had the sandy walls of the water pit reinforced with reeds from the riverbed and Bobbie had a woven mat of dead cattail leaves ready to cover the pit.

The smell of baking bread was maddening, and Jane had taken the last of her eight loaves back to the truck to be squirreled away in her pantry.

Matt came over to the fire looking for a handout. Bobbie was heating some water in a kettle and was about ready to make a big jar of pour-over coffee heavy with honey purchased at Chaffee.

"Jane is bringing down something to eat for breakfast," Bobbie said. "If you will tell Rona Ti to come back to the fire we will soon be ready to eat."

Rona Ti talked excitedly about seeing something in an open area in the cattails under a riverbank overhang. It took Matt most of the way back to figure out that she had been watching a new born calf not far from where the horses were grazing.

Baby animals never fail to catch the attention of a woman, Matt thought.

Bobbie was pouring coffee into four big mugs. The smell of coffee filled the air and it held Matt's attention.

"I hope we get to have a little of your fresh bread with the coffee I smell," Matt said.

"Not only do you get fresh bread with your coffee," Jane said, "I brought down canned apple butter to go with the bread."

Matt leaned back against a pile of sand and balanced a second cup of coffee on his chest. Bobbie stretched out beside him. His stomach was full, the air was cool, and they had more water than they needed. Things were good.

Jane had returned to the truck with the leftovers and Rona Ti started back to the horses. Matt was considering a little romance when Rona Ti tripped over the calf and it ran bawling toward the river bed. The alarm cry of the calf was answered by an old cow out in the reed patch. An excited cow came running to protect her calf.

Rona Ti quickly untied the horse hobbles, climbed aboard the smallest of the three horses, and hurried them toward the truck. The calf continued to bawl and the nervous old cow stomped her feet and snorted as she circled the calf.

Matt wasn't surprised at the behavior of the cow, he had seen it before, but he was surprised when a monstrosity of a bull came thrashing out of the brush not more than ten feet from where he sat. He watched the bull's headlong charge to the little patch of trampled reeds where the cow and calf shook with excitement. Matt smiled at the big brute throwing his weight around.

The bull was expecting to find something to knock down, and when he found nothing he muscled the cow out of his way and sniffed at the calf. Smelling nothing, he butted the calf over, and once more he forced the cow to give way to his charge. It was then that the bull noticed the fire.

By the time the bull got to the fire, Rona Ti and Jane had finished loading the truck. Seeing nothing else to fight, the angry bull gored the burning branches and threw them high in the air with his powerful neck muscles. He gouged with his horns and stomped with his forelegs until he had nothing left to attack. The wild-eyed beast was breathing heavily and drool from his nose and mouth sizzled as it dripped onto hot coals. He was straining to find something solid to hit.

Matt and Jane had worked lots of cattle, and they feared neither bulls nor cows. For the most part they didn't even respect the species. Bulls were prone to bluff with humans; however, they might fight another bull to the death. Because he understood this, Matt wasn't in any particular hurry. He expected this bull to be mostly bluff.

Jane agreed with Matt but she was more apt to notice individual differences. She saw a massive head covered with black, curly hair which extended down his neck and over his back. His horns grew out, curved forward, and then turned up. With his head held high he was as tall as Matt, and when he held up his tail like a little flag, he was sending a warning of his intent. What Matt and Jane didn't know was that this old brute made a living out of considering everything his enemy. He charged anything that he couldn't identify.

Matt was lucky to be walking up hill because the charge was a little slower and the bull had less lifting power with his head. As the bull closed in Matt turned and clattered the kettle against the oven thinking it would turn the animal from his charge. It didn't.

The bull caught Matt below the knees and flung him over his back. The oven and kettle flew into the air, and the clatter agitated the beast even more. Then, he turned his anger on Jane. Jane ducked under the horns, but he stepped on the back of her leg as he charged by. The bull caught sight of movement as Matt clambered to his feet.

Matt had no time to get out of the way, and once more he was thrown high into the air. He was lucky to fit between the points of the bull's horns. Unfortunately, Matt landed flat on his back and the jolt deflated his lungs. The bull spun around and lunged forward pinning Matt to the ground. The brute was about to put his horns to work when Jane yelled but it wasn't loud enough. Her leg hurt so that she couldn't lift herself off the ground. Bobbie put her hands over her face and turned away. She was frozen with fear.

Neither Bobbie nor Jane saw Rona Ti running down the hill pointing Matt's big rifle at the bull. She pulled back on the bolt feeding a shell into the chamber the same way that Matt had done it, and she squeezed the trigger. The recoil knocked her back on her bottom, but her shot landed neck high between the two shoulder blades, and the bull dropped on Matt.

They sat for a long moment trying to catch their breath. Matt pushed the animal's head to one side and slowly got to his feet. He removed his shirt, shook off the sand, and used it to wipe his face. He was covered with blood and slobbers from the old bull.

"Is anyone hurt," he asked, expecting to hear nothing.

Rona Ti pointed at Jane.

"Him stand on Jane."

Matt carried Jane up the hill to the truck where Bobbie cleaned Jane's wound with soap and water. After applying antiseptic she bandaged the wound.

"You have a bad scrape leading into a bleeding cut on the back of your thigh, but the worst part is the deep bruise down in the muscle. You're going to have to keep off your leg for several days."

"How am I going to get my work done?" Jane asked.

"I watch, I do work," Rona Ti answered.

Rona Ti was embarrassed and she looked down when her comments were followed by praise for ending the attack by the big bull. In her mind she was taking the gun to Matt, and the shot that killed the bull was probably an accident. At any rate, she remembered being knocked over backward, and she would show more respect for guns in the future.

"What about the bull?" Bobbie asked. "Do we just leave it to rot or are we going to do something with it?"

"That old devil will be as tough as saddle leather to eat," Jane said "But, even if he is old and tough, there will be a few good cuts of meat on him. And, Haze mentioned something about dogs. They have to eat something, and let's not forget about leather and horns."

"I can use the wench to pull him up here, but we will never get him dressed before the heat of the day. We'll have to get him back to the overpass to work on him and it will cost us an extra day. What will Haze think?"

No one answered so Rona Ti spoke up.

"Dark man like Jane plenty much. Jane damage leg, no problem."

The sun was up and the heat was starting to build causing Matt to be in a hurry. Bobbie and Rona Ti helped him hook the 'A' frame to the chassis. This saved an hour just screwing nuts and bolts together. After the frame was in place, Matt pulled the truck around so it was straight with the dead animal and he winched the big bull up to the edge of the road. He lifted the animal well off the ground so it was in position to be field dressed.

By noon they were back under the overpass, the bull was skinned and quartered, and the meat was hung and wrapped with cloth. The organs were cleaned, sliced, and put in a big pot to cook over a new fire. Most of this was done for Pete's dogs.

Bobbie helped Matt with the skin and horns and Rona Ti fanned Jane in the back of the truck.

Haze didn't knock before he looked in the door.

"What happened to you?" Haze asked, quietly.

"You warned us about the bull and sure enough one charged us. I ducked under his horns but he stepped on the back of my leg."

"Did it break the skin?"

"Yes," Jane admitted, "and there's a big bruise under it."

"Let me look at it," Haze said, not waiting for an invitation.

He opened the front of her trousers and rolled Jane over on her stomach. Haze pulled her trousers over her hips and down to her feet. Very gently he unwrapped the bandage.

After feeling the area around the wound he asked, "Did you clean the wound with soap and water?"

"Yes, and Bobbie put on an antiseptic. How does it look now?" Jane asked.

"Bobbie did the right things," he said, "but there be redness around the cut and it be deep and seepin' when I push on it."

"Don't push too hard, it hurts a lot," Jane cautioned.

Haze was talking to himself.

"I got antibiotic medicine that fights infection and speeds up the healing. It's got to be mixed, and that cut might need stitches to close. I can't get it here sooner than sundown."

Matt stuck his head in the door.

"Haze, I thought I heard your voice. I'm glad you came by. We have a batch of meat for you and your dogs. A bull got to us by the river and we had to kill it. And another thing, did you see this storm brewing up in the south?"

Haze followed Matt to the top of the overpass. It was unbearably hot and they had to shield their eyes to focus at a distance.

"We're in for a big blow," Haze said. "What we be lookin' at be a wall of dust just ahead of a wind storm. It's about two hours away. It be up to you, but I think we should move Jane up to my place so I can get some medicine on her leg. I can't get there and back before the storm hits, but you can in your truck."

"It can't wait until tomorrow?" Matt asked.

"Blood poisoning," Haze said, seriously. "It goes with wounds caused by animals. You fight blood poisoning real fast."

Matt made his decision.

"Then we get her to where the medicine is," he said.

Haze had one more bit of advice.

"One last thing, get everything covered and all the cracks plugged, because every crack, no matter how small, is going to let in dust."

It took half-an-hour to get Jane, Haze, and the meat to the Haze council canopy. After everything was unloaded Haze gave Matt a stack of large plastic sheets to cover the truck and horse trailer.

As Matt left town the wall of red dust was blotting out half of the southwestern sky. Strong winds had picked up as he pulled his truck into position under the overpass.

Matt and the women had to rush, but the big sheets of plastic were in place and tied down by the time the wall of dust hit. The wind blew, the plastic sheets flapped, and Matt understood about dust getting into everything. He hoped he hadn't forgotten anything. But he had. In their rush to get ready for the storm Matt had forgotten about Jane.

Chapter 3

Haze swung Jane over his shoulder like a sack of potatoes, and he jogged up the street to the most dilapidated, beat up, old shack on the street.

Jane didn't know what she had expected, but it certainly wasn't this. Part of the front porch was still intact and it extended over the driveway. The rest of the porch had broken loose and swung into the garage door below. To Jane, it was not only a hovel but it was falling apart and it leaned heavily to one side. Pete's house looked like a death trap.

Jane gave Haze a halfhearted smile as he lowered her to the porch. He took care not to bump her injured leg as he placed her on an old, canvas, porch chair.

The man, Jane thought, *is certainly a mystery, and that must be how he wants it.*

"That area to the southeast be Tinker Prison," Haze said, pointing. "That be your landmark. I'm gonna get you some medicine and I need to get the meat inside. Don't touch anything."

At first glance, the view beyond Tinker was a barren,

flat land as far as Jane could see. Looking a little closer she could see that it wasn't flat at all. She saw rolling hills with the remains of human activity firmly etched in the red clay hardpan, and far to the left and not so far out she could see a large pile of gray that must have been the building Haze pointed out.

Jane could see that Tinker Prison was a small part of something much larger. *At one time*, Jane thought, *that whole place was an air force base of several hundred acres. Those concrete paths were where planes landed and the buildings must have been immense. Hundreds of years of neglect, looting, and desert weather left nothing but a few foundations.*

Minutes later Haze returned to the porch and handed Jane two pills and a cup of water.

"The pills be for pain. They be makin' you sleep. When you wake up you'll be inside. Don't be surprised at what you see.

"The storm be almost here. It be moving faster than usual."

He spoke softly, and he was no longer speaking to Jane.

At the front door, Haze closed hidden switches. He opened the door, and immediately, two black Great Danes stepped into the doorway. Haze ushered the dogs outside, and he proceeded into the house turning off switches as he went. Each dog sniffed of Jane before they disappeared down the steps to check their territory.

Jane dozed as Haze carried her to a bedroom

somewhere in the house and situated her face down in the middle of a bed.

"Albedo," Pete said, "Send the medical drone. The girl be hurt."

"Pete," Albedo answered, "Where did you find a girl?"

"She be out on the hardtop road. Her leg be bleedin'."

"Pete, did you shoot her?"

"Albedo, she be stepped on by a bull down at the river bed. She ain't alone."

"Pete, adjust the video so that I might watch what you and the drone are doing.

"Okay, expose her wound and clean it with medicated soap and water from the medicine room. Be sure the bed is low enough for the drone to work. The medical drone is ready to help when you are finished."

"Albedo, I might fight these people if I decide to keep this one. You know I be needin' a woman for me. What be you're thoughts?"

"Pete, is she from the desert or is she passing through?"

"People in a truck be on their way to the west coast, but I be thinkin' they could stay with us. It ain't like we be short of room."

"Pete, the drone is finished stitching closed the wound. It was not deep but the bruise is. Take her to another bedroom with dry sheets. When she wakes up you might want to ask her if she and her people want to stay with us while she recuperates. If they are good people let the choice be theirs."

"Albedo, that be the proper way I guess."

One at a time Pete lifted Jane's arms and tied her wrists to the bed frame. She wasn't going to understand her situation when she awoke.

Jane was woozy when she opened her eyes.

"Where am I and why am I tied to a bed?" Jane asked, slowly.

"You be in my place," Pete said. "And I got to be sure you stay put while I ain't here to watch you. There be things you got to stay out of."

"Why?" Jane asked.

"Traps," Haze answered, "and other things."

"I don't have to be tied to a bed," Jane said. "I won't bother anything. I do what I'm told."

"Like you did in the truck," Pete said, sarcastically. "You cut out in that truck and left me and the horse for dead."

Haze made his point and Jane had no reply.

"The storm will hit before I get back," Haze continued, "but don't panic. This place will take whatever it's got."

"Where are we anyway?" Jane asked. "This can't be the inside of that old house."

"You might be surprised," Pete said, as he turned to leave.

Whirring and buzzing sounds followed shortly after Pete's departure. All sound ended for Jane with the sound of a heavy door opening and closing.

Jane looked around for a window. She recalled the big dark dirt cloud that was about to engulf the house. *A storm like that might blow this place over*, Jane thought. *I should be able to hear the wind and feel the house shake. The dirt was so thick in the air that it blocked out the sun, and*

I can't even hear a door rattle. How are those two big dogs making out, and how's Matt taking all this?

After a few minutes Jane lost interest in the storm, and she felt drowsy. The room was dark and she had nothing to hold her attention so she allowed herself to relax and sleep.

When Jane opened her eyes everything looked the same. She couldn't tell if it was day or night. Her wrists were still tied to the bed and she was covered by a white sheet. She flexed her injured leg, although it was sore it felt good to move it. She kicked off the sheet and discovered a different kind of bandage on her leg.

Jane turned toward the doorway and saw Haze perched on his heels in a rocking chair. It was too dark to see his eyes but she could feel them looking at her as he quietly tilted forward and back.

How long has he been there?

"Mr. Haze, could you free my hands and help me put on my pants," Jane said.

His reply was almost absentminded.

"I be thinkin' on it."

"Am I safe here?"

Haze was still in his preoccupied trance.

"Safe? This be the desert!"

Haze stepped out of his rocking chair and looked at Jane.

"You're going to be mean to me aren't you?" Jane said.

"No," Haze mumbled. "I be wonderin' what to do about you and your people."

Haze slowly sat on the edge of Jane's bed and lifted

her lower leg. He checked the bandage and found it to be tight and he saw that her wound wasn't bleeding through the gauze.

"Does your wound hurt when I lift your leg?"

"Not much."

There will be time to talk, Jane thought, *and I might be able to talk him out of this.*

"Mr. Haze, what is your first name?" Jane asked.

"Pete.

After a long moment of silence Pete looked up.

"Your injury ain't that bad. I just wanted to know if you be worth keepin'."

Haze was groggy from lack of sleep, and his thoughts weren't entirely clear.

"And what did you decide?" Jane asked.

She be down right pretty, Pete thought, *but what if she commenced to blubberin' if something happened to her brother. Could I trust her? If I couldn't trust her I'd have to get rid of her and what would be gained. How do I get her to want to stay with me? I don't care what Patch said, a women ain't gonna make you weak. Maybe it's time to trust someone. If they decide to go I ain't never gonna have a woman of my own.*

"I think you be nice to look at," Pete said.

Pete turned up the light a little and Jane saw a hint of Pete's face. It was still too dark to see details, but he had trimmed back his hair and shaved. She fancied seeing a nice face with no scars and he was young?

Pete came out of his trance when he heard Jane voice.

"Pete, could I ask a favor?" Jane said, softly.

"Yeah, probably."

"I know you're struggling with what to do with me, but I know how it's going to turn out. So, first, I give you permission to do with me what you will as long as you don't hurt me. Second, since you have my permission it's no longer necessary to have my wrists tied to the bed."

Pete was surprised.

"Why are you telling me this?"

"Well, I've never been with a man before, and I don't want the first time to be something bad."

"I don't know what you be thinkin', but this ain't just about you. I be wonderin' about your whole family."

Pete reached up to cut the bonds that held Jane's wrists.

"I've never been with a woman neither," Pete said. "But I don't think of it as bein' somethin' bad."

Pete left the room and promptly returned with Jane's clothing, but Jane didn't look at what he was holding. She was fascinated by his face.

"Pete, without all the hair and whiskers to hide behind, you have a nice face. I'm going to have to apologize for my thoughts. I thought you were trying to hide some terrible scar. Why all the hair?"

"Scars be there," Pete admitted, "but I wasn't hidin' anything. Had no reason to cut it."

Jane felt that she had misunderstood her situation.

"Listen, what did you mean when you told Matt that you coveted his sister? Did it mean that you wanted me for your own or did it mean that you just wanted to use me for a while?"

"I don't know," Pete said. "I think it meant I might talk myself into keepin' you here as my woman."

"Is that why you tied me in bed?" Jane asked.

"What I told you about traps be true," Pete said. "On the other hand, I didn't know if you could be trusted if it weren't your idea to stay. Then it came to me that I got enough enemies without addin' any more, so what I said holds. Stay as long as you want."

Jane was quiet while she studied Haze and thought about what she should do. Jane saw something she liked in this young man.

"Pete, do you believe in love at first sight?"

"No," Pete answered.

"What if I reminded you that I'm not tied now, and I don't take it back."

Pete looked down.

"And tomorrow you leave."

"We don't have to go tomorrow," Jane said, "and when we do go there's no reason why you couldn't go with us if you felt like it. A lot depends on if you can put your feelings into words. How do you feel about me now?"

Haze thought a minute.

"I'd like for you to want to stay here."

It was obvious that Haze was uncomfortable talking about such things because he looked down when he spoke.

"I guess you be thinkin' about love or marryin' up with someone," Pete said. "I don't think it gets hold of a person that fast. The men talked about such as that, and they said too much woman chitchat made a person weak, and weak people don't run in the desert."

"Never-the-less, that's what it takes for a woman to

want to be with a man," Jane said. "That's what we're getting at here isn't it? A woman that wanted to stay with one man."

Haze didn't answer.

"One of the reasons why I left our part of the country," Jane said, "was that all the young men were taken. I didn't want to be an old maid, and I didn't want to be a breeder girl. I told myself when we left, if I find someone, fine, and if I don't at least I'll see the country. Well, I found you. And, I liked you because you saved us from bad people, and you helped us get the truck this far, and just now you couldn't be mean to me. And, now that I have seen your face and I know more about how you think I don't mind telling you that I'm starting to have feelings for you.

"Now then, Mr. Haze, do you want me to spend my life with you or not?"

Jane watched Pete closely as he started.

"A long time ago, before my fathers be gone, one of them thought he be teachin' some good advice. He told me, 'Life in these parts be too hard for a normal woman. If they survive at all they'll be hard-hearted and meaner than a desert wasp. So there probably ain't none left. But, if I'm wrong and a stray wanders in here, and if by chance she ain't too dumb, or too ugly, ask her to be your wife because that's the one thing that'll keep her from running off when she gets tired of you. If, by chance, you find a pretty one, ask her to be your wife but you tell her you love her first, because that's the one thing that'll keep someone better than you from taking her away from you.' I didn't know what he be talking about until now."

Haze took a moment to get his thoughts together.

"I ain't sure about many things but I'm sure about

bein' afraid of losing you. So I tied you to the bed. If it be love that I feel, and it most likely is, I probably won't talk about it a lot, but I'll show you everyday. I'd be proud for you to be my wife."

It wasn't quite what Jane expected but it was good enough.

"I'd be happy to be your wife."

Occasionally an event takes over the mind preventing memories from sorting out properly. And, so it was with Pete as he ran through the worst windstorm the desert had to offer and he barely noticed.

Pete remembered the silhouette of Jane standing in the doorway, and he remembered holding this pretty young woman in his arms, and he remembered that she gave herself to him so completely that it took his breath away, but now it was time to think about the wind and dirt.

Pete was running on one of his regular trails. Normally he was alert and watchful but today his head was full of other things.

Grandpa always be the lucky one, Pete thought, *but last night with Jane, it be my turn, and she talked like she be the lucky one. I hope I didn't hurt her, she wouldn't let go of me. I've got to alter my way of thinkin' or I'll drive her away. She already changed and I have to meet her half way. I wish Ma could see how pretty she be and there be no doubt that she wanted me just as much as I wanted her.*

Pete caught himself smiling. She had whispered funny things in his ear when she thought he was sleeping.

"How can a body be expected to sleep with that kind of thing going on?"

Jane needs to have her bible, Pete thought. *What could that be about?*

They ain't gonna believe their eyes. Ain't nothin' movin' in Haze Territory and the dogs be quiet. Looks like the storm changed a few things. Anything blockin' the wind got a big drift of dirt and debris behind it. Looks to be a few buildings pushed over.

Pete was running faster now. He wanted to get to the overpass road before it got light. *They be started to clean dust out of their truck.*

Pete stepped under the plastic sheet.

"We got drifts of dirt everywhere and buildings be blown away, but there ain't no signs of Drummonds or the others. Jane ain't bad hurt and she wants her bible. Do you want me to tell Jane anything?"

"Yes," Bobbie said. "We have the inside of the truck clean and I have some food packed up for you."

On his way out Pete yelled at Matt.

"Come up to my place for dinner tonight. Don't bring anything."

Now I gotta get back and introduce Jane to Albedo.

Chapter 4

Jane had little to say as Pete ushered her into the computer room. She gave her name, numbers from one to ten, and the alphabet, which satisfied Albedo's requirements for recognition.

Jane had questions for the computer.

"Albedo."

"Yes, Jane."

"Would it bother you if I asked you a bunch of questions?

"No, Jane. I would be pleased to talk with you about anything at any time in any room."

"Albedo," Pete said, "can talk to everyone in every room all at the same time, and that be just the start of what he can do. He knows everything worth knowin'. Albedo be like a father and the drones be brothers. They kept me goin' after Ma left."

"Jane."

"Yes, Albedo."

"There are many things that we should discuss. We might want to have a long conversation later today. I think

Pete asked the rest of your family here for your evening meal so I need to discuss food for them. I will help the kitchen drone make a menu."

Pete assembled his new family on the porch.

"Don't touch anything until you understand it," he warned.

Pete led his new family past a series of switches, numbered button panels, and doors. Strange things happened at each stop. Obstacles moved out of the way, walls dropped into place, other walls moved to the side, and a tangle of broken construction material suddenly became a clear path to the back of the house.

Pete punched a code into a button panel and the back wall became a double sliding door. A light came on as the door opened and they could see to step into a small, square room with another lighted panel by the door. Pete pushed a key into a small slot and turned it. The doors closed. He pushed another button and the square room started to drop.

"The box that we're in is an elevator, and below us be a fallout shelter."

Jane ushered Matt, Bobbie, and Rona Ti into a room filled with tables and chairs. One table had settings for five.

Partially separated from the dining area was a large kitchen the likes of which the Blacktowers had never seen. A little kitchen drone took one guest at a time to a specific chair and seated them.

"Jane, what is Pete fixing and why aren't you helping?"

"He hasn't let me in on everything yet. I think I have a lot to learn because everything is so different. He said to be patient and he would show all of us at the same time."

"So you're married now," Matt said. "The way you're smiling, does he treat you the way you wanted to be treated?"

"Matt, what are you asking? Was this my idea or his? I saw how happy you and Bobby were and I thought it was my turn."

"Poppa ordered me to watch after you," Matt said, "and I wanted to hear it from you."

"Well," Jane said, with a smile, "Pete treated me like a bride expects to be treated. Actually I was afraid I had hurt him a time or two."

Matt laughed.

"Then I pass my responsibility to Pete. He sounds capable."

Bobbie whispered in Jane's ear.

"Don't let him fool you. Matt was worried that Pete might be too intense for you."

"Pete and Matt are a lot alike," Jane said. "I think that will help me understand Pete."

The food was hot and steamy when the kitchen drone brought it to the table.

"I wanted you to taste a sample of what I have, but I'm never sure how any one item will taste so I brought out a variety. This food was preserved a long time ago and most of it's still fairly good because it was kept cold, dry and dark. Albedo, can you add anything?"

"Yes, Pete, I can and I will keep my remarks short.

In most cases this food was over preserved because it extended the shelf life almost indefinitely. Some said it doesn't taste as good as fresh food, others like it better.

"Completely prepared meals were made and preserved for special people by the best cooks in the country at that time, and that is what will be on the table for you."

The drone placed a partitioned dish with precooked food before each person, and Pete put several single dishes in the center of the table.

"If there be too much or if you don't like somethin' don't eat it, my dogs like it all. And, don't ask what these things be because I don't know. Save a little room for something special at the end."

Matt talked with his mouth full.

"I have to say it's different, but tasty. How much do you have?"

"A lot of this kind of thing be in the freezers. I be raised on it, and if this be all you got to eat you eventually get tired of it."

"How was it kept from spoiling?" Bobbie asked.

"Albedo." Pete said.

"The majority of our food was canned in glass or in metal cans," Albedo said.

"Right now," Pete said. "I got one more thing for you to try."

Pete opened a box in the center of the table, and he scooped out five servings of brown stuff. Next, he spooned on a thick white layer and he popped a red thing on top.

"This be dessert. They call it chocolate ice cream."

"For several years I lived in a wall city with the rich

people," Bobbie said, "and believe me they had nothing like this. You say it's how old?"

"It be nearly five-hundred years old.

"This place," Pete continued, "ain't nothin' but an underground military post, and what you see from here be a small part of it. I'll show you around in a few minutes.

After dessert Albedo and Pete explained the story of the shelter.

"To me, it be an oasis in the middle of a wasteland," Pete said. "It be all I've got. So from now on my territory will be known as Haze-Blacktower Territory. And, you need to be able to tell our story to the ones that follow."

Chapter 5

"The rest of this place is hard to describe," Pete said, "so I think I should show you."

Inside cold storage the Blacktowers found the temperature to be uncomfortably cold. Pete pointed out an escape hatch and a trouble light switch to be used in emergencies.

"Don't ever let yourself get trapped in here. It's cold but it gets even colder in the next two lockers. If you can't open the door turn on the trouble light and count to thirty. If you don't hear help outside, push this button to blow the escape hatch in the door.

"How long could five people live off of this?" Matt asked.

Pete thought a minute.

"There's probably enough frozen meals for forty-five to fifty years or more. It would last quite a bit longer if you mixed in a little fresh food from the outside."

Pete led his guests out of the dining area to a lobby where he assigned sleeping rooms.

"The room across the way is Medical. The drone can

take care of anything from a common cold to complicated surgery. All medications be kept dry and frozen. Albedo says their shelf life hasn't started yet.

"Where did you get the electrical power?" Bobbie asked.

"Everything inside runs by atomic battery. Things what goes to the desert, like jeeps, needs a wet battery. I add water when I take them out of storage."

"We got a long dark hall to get to Tactical. Ain't much to see in Tactical because the only part I use is the surveillance system. From there we will go to the Motor Pool. We will keep your animals there."

"So many strange things here," Jane said. "How did the people know how to make them work?"

Pete considered how much to tell them.

"Everything in here be in common use five hundred years ago. Keep in mind, they walked on the moon, they transplanted organs from one person to another person, they went five miles deep in the ocean, and they rode in airplanes that flew faster than sound."

"How do you know all this?" Jane asked.

"From the video tapes that ain't got crumbly," Pete said. "Albedo can tell you more about the great tool makers if there be things you need to know."

"Albedo," Matt said. "Do you have someone on the outside to talk to?"

"Matt, I established and maintained contact with computers on the outside until the last of our satellites fell out of the sky."

Pete was walking and talking.

"We have to go down by the utility pod to get to

the motor pool from here. The utility pod has an escape tunnel out the back door."

As they entered the central room Matt saw trucks, jeeps, and a rack full of different sized motorcycles. Scattered straw stems and the smell of livestock lingered on.

"I see you had farm animals put up in here a few years back," Matt said.

"Grandpa brought cattle and horses from Chaffee when the prison was workin'," Pete said.

Pete stopped in front of a large plate glass window and looked inside.

"I got two small airplanes parked in this room. With the help of Albedo and the Motor pool drone Grandpa and his two cousins got motorcycles fixed up and runnin'. I did the same with a jeep. If you got the interest I thought we might work on the airplanes."

"You mean so we could fly?"

"Yeah."

"I got the time if you do," Matt said, looking at Jane.

"I reckon once we learn about the wind we got flying under control."

"Where do you keep the fuel?"

"The things that I drive burn gasoline and most of it be stored in underground tanks away from the complex. The stored gasoline has a stabilizer that protects it until it be ready to use. I add a mixture from the storeroom for the jeep."

"How much gasoline do you have tucked away," Matt asked.

"I ain't sure what be stored here," Pete answered,

"but there be a lot put by in different places around the country."

"I guess an airplane will fly pretty fast don't it?"

"They will go a lot faster than your steamer truck but the air comin' out stinks and your truck don't smell. About sunup we can take out one of the jeeps and run my checkpoints. You can drive. Okay, the ammo dump and the gun range is around on the far side. In the morning before we make our rounds, you can each pick out the kind of gun you want to carry and I'll show you how to use it. You can practice all you want in the target range. We have lots of ammunition. Most of it be good."

That night in bed, Jane noticed that her new husband was restless.

"Pete, is something bothering you?"

"I feel edgy about something," Pete whispered.

"Is it me?"

"Some," Pete said. "There be things here and in the desert that you don't understand. When I was alone, I didn't worry about anything. Now I have people to worry about, and I think worry ain't a good thing to have. Am I wrong?"

"No," Jane said, "but you shouldn't worry about us. We can take care of ourselves."

"I can't show something like worry to my enemies. They'll see it as a weakness."

"You fought five-to-one odds with the Drummonds and you went out in that awful storm. If ever there was a person without worry it's you."

"I've come to terms with whatever be happenin' to me," Pete said. "I'll be killed in a fight with one of the clans. My worries be that one of you people will die because I failed you somehow . . . there be so many ways to die in the desert."

If you take the time to tell us, we will remember. We are not dumb people. If you want us to be like you, then you must teach us."

"We could be fighting with someone tomorrow, and I could be alone again tomorrow night."

"Like you, I've come to terms with my future," Jane said. "Last night I dreamed that I watched our children playing, a son and a daughter. You were standing by my side watching over us."

"This really be your dream?" Pete asked.

"Yes," Jane said, "every time I dozed off I had the same dream."

A flood of relief came over Pete.

"Then I will teach you and you will learn. You and your family will make Haze strong again. Dreams be a good sign."

Pete pulled Jane to him and leaned back on his pillow. She came to him eagerly and savored the warmth of a tender moment. Then Pete shuddered.

"Now what's wrong?"

Pete hesitated before answering.

"When I hold you like this I remember how close I came to doing the wrong thing. I had thoughts of forcing you to be my mate."

"I know you did. That's why I gave you permission. After that, it didn't make any difference what you did. I wasn't going to take a chance on losing you for doing something I wanted just as much as you did."

43

Chapter 6

The next morning they were finished with their coffee well before sunup. Pete was anxious for each person to arm themselves because the bandit clans feared Pete's weapons.

In the Ammo Dump Pete learned quickly that Matt and Jane were capable gun handlers. Bobbie on the other hand didn't like all the noise, and Rona Ti closed her eyes when she pulled the trigger. Pete found small caliber semiautomatic handguns for the girls to carry.

Pete emphasized his final point.

"Remember this one thing above all else don't ever trust the other clans . . . not even the women. They will shoot you if they have a bullet, they will cut your throat if they have a knife. In the past they have had problems keeping ammunition on hand. If they see you and don't shoot at you then they be out of ammo. Use this against them. They use their own children or their own wounds to make you forget where you are. They'll sacrifice anything to put a knife in your gut.

"If you should find one on the ground groveling up

to you, begging for help the kindest thing you can do is put a bullet in his brain, then look for others sneaking in behind you. We don't ever take prisoners or wounded! If by chance you should ever mistakenly bring one in here . . I'll kill 'em."

To Matt, driving the jeep was worth the trip. As he headed west out of the city ruins, he marveled at the ease of control of the small, lightweight vehicle. The old steamer truck was so heavy that he had to put his shoulders into the steering, but the jeep could be guided with little more than a flick of the wrist.

What would this thing be like on a smooth surface? Matt thought. *It must be like driving a rain cloud.*

Pete let Matt have his fun before he put a stop to it. Pete remembered what it was like the first time he took a jeep out and today he had no reason for excessive caution. However, the sun was up and they still had roads to scan.

The riverbed was clear, the highway was empty to the west, the trail around the north side was free of sign, and the highways to the north and east were empty. This was what Pete expected.

If anyone comes in on us today, Pete thought, *it'll probably be the Drummonds, and they would come from the south.*

Matt came to a sliding stop in the middle of his campsite under the overpass. His thoughts were of horses.

"Do we have time to get the horses to the river to graze in the shade a little?" Matt asked.

"The wind is going to pick up today," Pete said, "but that shouldn't be a problem until later. We can take the horse trailer behind the jeep."

Matt pulled the jeep in place and both men slid out of the jeep thinking about the task at hand.

Glancing back, Pete become aware of the silhouette of an old man standing in a dusty halo of morning light and dust. He was several yards behind them.

"Matt don't move, and don't say anything. The old man behind us be a Clan Elder and he be unarmed. That means there be guns pointed at us."

Pete added a comment under his breath.

"Damn it, I never saw a thing! They came in under the cameras and here I stand empty handed."

The Elder spoke in the same breathless quiet way as Pete.

"I see you be a man now. Be you the head of the Haze Clan?"

"I guess I be that right enough, Elder. Grandpa Kyle be back east hunting down the rest of your people. We be Haze-Blacktower now. I am joined by the family of my wife, and they share in all that I have."

"It be good that you found someone. Growing old alone be bad for the digestion and the heart." A moment of silence passed before the old man continued. "We found your Ma walking in the desert eight year ago. Her thoughts be far away, and she wouldn't take water. When she passed on our women sewed her in white, and they put her grave in Haze Territory. They said prayers for her deliverance."

"Your women placed me in your debt," Pete said, respectfully. "What would you have in return?"

"I'd hear about my son, Sweet Brady Chastain, if you be knowin'" the Elder requested.

"Sweet Brady Chastain be helpin' this man and his women to cross the desert when they came under attack by five Drummonds near Chisholm Wells. I killed the Drummonds."

The Elder nodded his approval.

"Was he put underground?"

Pete nodded.

"Did you say a prayer of deliverance for him?"

"Yes, a prayer be said for each."

"What would you ask in return?" the old one asked.

"I would have killed the Drummonds anyway, and I don't ask favors for doing what's right for the dead."

"In all ways you sound like your Great Grandpa, and that speaks well for what you are, because he was one of the best desert men I ever did fight."

In a reverent tone the old man continued.

"Did Brady die well?"

"Brady was dead by the time I got there," Pete stated, "so I can't tell you."

Matt spoke up, and his voice fairly boomed in comparison to the others.

"I was tied up on the ground, and I couldn't see very well but I could hear. Brady died without making a sound." Matt didn't mention that Brady's mouth was tied shut.

"I'm goin' to make your women forever free from the bullets of my sons because I ain't beholdin' to any man. Just you remember, I can speak for what's mine but I don't carry much influence with the young ones. They think I live too much in the past."

Pete's reply was quick.

"Then let them beware."

"This also be my warning to them," the Elder said, changing his tone, "but the young ones grow tired of having nothing. They think that the Haze Clan has much that they should share. They call you selfish. Sometimes we are short of food or water and you must have extra, but you don't offer any to us.

"Consider ammunition, this is always something we could use. How many guns and bullets do you own? I think that you have many more than you can shoot. I think that you have gold and silver. I've seen your grandpa showing off his gold at the market in Chaffee."

Five or six of the younger Chastains were now creeping in on the two men by the jeep. One was standing on the back of the truck and one was behind the horse trailer.

Matt spoke a little too loud and a little too fast for the Chastains.

"Here you can have my old M-1, be careful, it's loaded."

That said he reached into the back of the jeep, grabbed the gun, and flipped it up to the young Chastain on the back of the truck. His actions were unexpected, and he continued to talk all the while.

"We have a little gold and some silver hidden in the back of the truck, and to be honest with you some of it belongs to you. We had contracted Sweet Brady Chastain to guide us to Tinker Prison, and he died before we could pay him."

Matt was up on the back of the truck before they could protest.

"If one of you will follow me into the back of my truck, I'll be glad to get it for you."

Matt lifted a rack of dried roots and spices from the wall and placed it on the floor. He lifted a sliding panel in the wall and started to put in his hand when the young man in black stopped him. Matt smiled and backed away.

"Here, let me at that," the young man said, but another young man standing in the door stopped him. "He be too willing. There be a trap in that hole, you fool. Make him do it."

The anxious one waved Matt forward.

Matt stepped up to the wall, rolled up his sleeve, and lifted the panel. Matt frowned as he placed his hand in the opening. He turned and twisted his hand and arm as he reached down into the hiding place. He tickled the coins with his finger making a clinking sound. Matt started to pull out his hand, but he stopped and grimaced.

Excitement was building in the young Chastain.

"Hurry up, I want to see it."

Matt's voice carried out the back of the truck.

"I can't go too fast, I have to work my hand by the barbs. Some of them are triggers that will shoot a sharp blade into my wrist. I could lose a hand!"

The kid's face was covered, but his eyes gave away his eagerness. He inched closer as the fellow in the door looked out toward the jeep. One of his brothers had grabbed Pete's fast shooting quiet gun.

In a flash Matt pulled the revolver from its hiding place and put a bullet in the eye of the young Bandit watching him. Next he dropped the cautious Chastain standing in the doorway.

Pete fell to the ground as Matt came rolling and shooting out the door. The young Chastain covering Pete looked for a place to hide.

The boy with Matt's gun stood on the tailgate squeezing the trigger but nothing happened. The safety was on.

Pete pulled a tiny gun from inside his belt and ended the young man's confusion. The last two lads were into their head-down-shuffle as Matt regained his M-1. They were out of sight before he could shoot. Pete had picked up his automatic weapon, and thought for a moment about giving chase but the thought passed as he saw Matt level his rifle at the old man.

"Matt," Pete said, "the Elder is unarmed, and gun butts of his sons be on the ground. They ain't in this fight."

Matt lowered the M-1 and returned to the truck to collect the remainder of the money that he owed to Brady. He walked out to the old man and placed it in his hand.

"What I told you was the truth. Like you, I'm beholding to no man. It's a shame that the wisdom of an Elder was wasted. Children shouldn't play at war. You would be wise to collect your dead and wounded and be gone."

The Chastains picked up their dead and left.

Pete watched closely as the Chastains retreated. They had used a new route into his territory, and he would have to see that it was taken away from them.

Matt continued with his plans to tend to the horses while Pete followed the Chastains.

In a matter of minutes his animals were watered and grazing by the river. Matt had no chores to fill his time while the horses fed, so he pulled the M-1 over his shoulder, picked up a pair of field glasses, and looked for a high place to set and keep watch.

An hour passed, then two and Matt continued to study his surroundings. He was surprised by Pete's voice.

"Anything movin' out there?"

"I think I see smoke up the riverbed," Matt said, handing the glasses to Pete.

"You're right, it be smoke," Pete said. "Most likely Indians way up north. One of my dads called Blade, could be his people. His real first name be Dull Knife, didn't like his name much."

Pete concentrated on the horizon to the south.

"Did you notice anything strange about the fight with the Chastains?"

"They didn't fire any shots," Matt said.

"Exactly, I think the whole thing be set up by the Elder to get their hands on ammunition. I doubt they had any concern about my mother or Sweet Brady Chastain for that matter. They let the lure of gold alter their plan and it made a strong position weak. How did you manage to pull a gun on them?"

"Our Old Man put a revolver on top of the money he gave us for the trip," Matt answered.

"You gotta trust the wisdom of the old ones."

Chapter 7

By midday Matt and Pete had returned the horses to the protection of the overpass. Matt stretched out in the truck cab and Pete sat on the tailgate. Small talk was over and the men slept.

Matt awoke with a growling stomach. He felt around through the cab's rear window and located the jar that Jane used to store jerky. *A cup of water and a biscuit would go good with a hank of jerky,* Matt thought. *I should wait until we go back to the shelter*

In the back of the truck Matt found what he was looking for, and he ate his small snack.

I wonder where Pete went, Matt thought. He isn't with the horses or the jeep. Why would he leave the truck without waking me up.

From the concrete overpass above the truck Pete call to Matt.

"Matt, did you hear anything?"

"No," Matt answered. "I was getting something to eat out of the truck box. Was it me that you heard?"

Pete dropped down from the overpass, and he ate and

drank while he listened. He had picked up vibrations of something at the edge of his sense of hearing.

Ten minutes passed and neither man moved.

"I thought I heard a thump-like sound to the north," Pete said, "I ain't sure because sound don't travel good durin' the hot part of the day not like it does at night."

"We got a south breeze which doesn't help," Matt said.

Pete put a finger to his lips and cocked his head to one side.

"There it be again an explosion and small caliber shots bein' fired. It's coming from the shelter!"

Matt and Pete leaped into the jeep and they roared up the on-ramp. Pete loaded a belt of ammo into the machine gun mounted on top while Matt drove. For the first time Matt felt the real heat of the sun beating down and he was sweating profusely. When the road leveled out Pete reached for the radio switch.

Immediately they heard Jane's panicky call for help.

"Pete! Matt! If you can hear me answer back right now! Someone is trying to blow us up, over!"

"Jane, did anyone get hurt?" Pete said.

"Pete, thank God! Where have you been? Those people you were fighting this morning came back, and they blew up your house, and I think you lost your elevator, over!

"Jane, we be at the river with the horses, and we just now picked up some sounds like gun fire. I take it you didn't get hurt, we be on our way as fast as we can, over!"

"Pete, we were looking at the computers trying to keep track of you and Matt when we got rocked by a big bomb blast. Bobbie and Rona Ti went out the utility pod exit, and right now, they're shooting at both ends of a drainage culvert that's got bandits hiding inside, over!"

"Did any of the Chastains get inside the shelter? Over!"

"I don't know," Jane answered. "Big door-like things came down out of the ceiling and closed off the main halls after the explosion. I got one of your cameras turned to cover the house up above, and it looks like your traps caught one or two raiders at the front door, but they was followed in by at least two more. One managed to blow away the front of the house. A few minutes later another explosion came from deep inside. There's lots of damage but it's too dark to see details, over."

"Have you seen my dogs? Over."

"They left with Bobbie and Rona Ti, and they caught one of the guys out in the street. He's still there. The last I saw of them they were running after a second fellow out in the flat land. I might be wrong, but the clan stopped shooting. I think they're out of bullets. They're throwing explosives to keep the girls back, and they're keeping out of sight. What do you want us to do? Over."

"You be doing the right things, use your cameras to look around at some of the high points. You should be able to see an old man watchin' from a hill top, over."

"Give me a minute," Jane said. "I have to change the camera angles, and I have to refocus. I think I've got something about a mile east of here. He's an old man with a walking stick. I see kids behind him, over."

"We be about to get in on the fightin' at the culvert," Pete said. "I can see Bobbie from here. Keep the old man in sight, out."

As soon as the jeep pulled into view the Chastains lit the fuses on their explosives. They charged out of either end of the culvert mindless of the chatter of Pete's machine gun. Two of the Chastains managed to launch their hand bombs at Rona Ti and Bobbie. The rest went down with bombs in their hands. None of the Chastain invaders survived.

"Jane," Pete said. "Are you there? Over."

"I'm here. What was all that noise? Over."

"We be helpin' at the culvert. Bobbie and Rona Ti be okay. The real problem be that old man. Can you still see him? Over."

"Yes," Jane said. "He turned away and he and a couple of young ones are walking kind of slow to the northeast, over."

"I'm gonna fire a burst in his direction," Pete said. "Tell me where the bullets land and how he handles it, over."

Pete pulled up his sights and fixed them at a thousand yards. He fired several bursts at the top of the hill where the old man was supposed to be.

"He heard the bullets hit," Jane said. "You got him to stop and look around. From the direction he was looking you need to go to the left and farther out. He's walking again, over."

Pete adjusted his sights and fired.

"You went right over his head. He took a dive and covered up his head. Now he's trying to run, over."

Pete waited several seconds and fired two long bursts, one to the left and one to the right.

"You're kicking up dirt all around him, and he acts as though he doesn't know which way to go. He dropped his walking stick and he found some running speed from somewhere. He's going to be out of sight behind a hill in a second or two, over."

Pete continued to shoot over the top of the hill until his ammunition belt was empty.

"Jane, did I get the old man? Over."

"Not as far as I could see," Jane said. "You gave him something to think about. Are you going after him? Over."

Pete was quiet for a minute.

"Later maybe, over."

"What was this about anyway? Over."

Pete was angry with himself.

"I didn't follow my own advice, I let a Chastain Elder talk at the truck, and he and a gang of kids got the drop on us. I thought he wanted to know about Brady, but when the talkin' was over his kids came in on us and we had to gun down four of 'em. My second mistake was stoppin' Matt from finishin' the job.

"I had 'em on the run and they still came back on us."

While Matt pulled the dead raiders out of the ditch Pete returned the jeep to the motor pool and attached a trailer. At the top of a hill east of the shelter Pete found one of the Elder's dead kids to load in his trailer, but the old man was gone. The rest of the dead Chastains were taken to the burial pits.

Pete thought it was necessary to look for openings in the demolished house above the shelter before he lost daylight.

I've got to be sure the damaged area is secure, Pete

thought, *I've got to lock down any weakness. Ain't no way of knowing if the Chastains can git at us. I wonder if Matt has any ideas.*

Matt examined the damage around the outside of the deceptive old house while Pete carefully made his way through the front door into the main hall.

Pete's stared at the damaged upper part of the elevator.

It ain't never gonna run again, Pete thought, *and the elevator shaft has to be a weakness that the Chastains can pick at until they get inside.*

Pete wanted a closer look at the lower end of the shaft. He carefully worked his way back to the fake wall which had fallen into a gapping hole in the floor at the end of the hall. He stretched himself out over the dislodged wall and peered into the rubble left by the shattered elevator box.

Pete raised himself to a crouching position and extended one leg toward the sliding door frame. Little by little he shifted his weight to the foot on the frame. Unexpectedly the frame dropped several inches and fell toward Pete. Pete rolled sideways and a small person jumped on top of him.

Chapter 8

Defend yourself, Pete thought, *then attack.*

The small man didn't move. The small body wasn't a man. Pete's attacker was a dead woman. *Most likely killed by the explosion in the elevator shaft,* Pete thought.

Matt looked into the back of the house through a gapping hole in the wall.

"Are you okay in there?" Matt asked.

"Matt, it's a good thing we weren't both in here," Pete said. "I got another body and it be a woman. She be messed up."

"Are you needing a rope?" Matt said.

"Yeah, she be tangled in the debris. I'd guess she lit the fuse and couldn't get away. There she squatted, trapped on top of who knows what, and she got herself blasted up into the rafters. She came back down with part of the ceiling"

"Give me a minute," Matt said, "We got a rope in the jeep."

The body wasn't heavy but Pete felt awkward trying

to help lift the body. Foot holds had given away under his weight. He had no place to stand, so Pete left it up to Matt to lift the dead woman out of the collapsing old house.

Once more Pete looked into the mass of twisted metal, broken concrete, and cable.

"Matt, while I'm in here I need to get down in the elevator shaft to see if anyone can get in there."

"Pete, you're gonna get trapped in the debris if you do. What's left of the ceiling and roof is about to drop on you right now."

The next sound that Matt heard was a loud groan then a powerful jolt as the roof came crushing down taking everything in its way to the first floor.

Matt returned to the shelter after taking the dead bomber woman to be with her people. In the motor pool Bobbie, Rona Ti, and Jane quizzed him relentlessly about the condition of the first floor. Questions were long and answers were short. Matt reminded them that the condition of the house could be assessed only when sunlight allowed him to see into the shadows.

All in all, Pete looked at the day as a good one. None of his people got hurt, his dogs were back, and as far as he was concerned the shelter could be fixed.

"Look at all the people that died today," Matt said. "They didn't actually know anything about this place."

"I wonder what the last two minutes were like for that woman that got blown up," Bobbie said. "Did she know she was going to die?"

"She did if she could see the fuse burning down," Matt said. "She was close to the charge, the poor thing was nearly blown in two. I thought I was gonna finish the job pulling her out of there."

"Her luck ran out and ours didn't," Pete said. "A ceiling beam came down right where I was standin'. Matt warned me and that probably made the difference."

"Pete," Jane said. "Tell me again how the main hall down here got closed off. I was watching the monitors, and I missed all that."

Pete led the way to one of the partition that dropped out of the ceilings.

"This place be designed to protect its people if ever an attack or accident happened."

Pete kicked the heavy steel divider.

"If the system be workin' a damaged area be sealed off when one of these steel panels drops out of the ceiling and settles into a groove in the floor. They put one of these things at the openin' into each living section. Only utility, the motor pool, and tactical be left open."

"We can't get into the food now, right?" Jane said, frowning. "I was just getting used to running water, and what about the rest rooms?"

Pete opened a panel at floor level and removed a crank handle.

"Every panel has one of these," Pete said. "The gear ratio be high because of the weight. It takes a lot of turns of the crank handle to pull the door up an inch."

Pete inserted the handle and gave it a few turns.

"Pullin' up the door panels will give you girls something to do while Matt and I finish a job or two."

"Where are you going?" Jane asked.

"Until now," Pete answered, "ain't none of the other

clans know about the connection between the shelter and the beat-up old house above us. Common knowledge be that we lived near Tinker Prison.

"The Elder has verified that they opened one of my doors, and he be lookin' over his shoulder for me because he knows that I know. To answer your question, we be on our way to prevent him from passin' on any of that information."

"Shouldn't we be leaving?" Matt asked.

"The Chastains got a couple of places. They'll most likely be in the one at the fork of two dry rivers. The other place got leveled by Grandpa Kyle. I'll give the old man a few hours of walkin' and thinkin' he be safe. We got plenty of time to find him in my jeep."

"How can a clan like them survive in a desert?" Matt asked

"In the old days a clan be connected to farm people at the edge of the desert. They supplied about half of what a clan needed and the other half came from trade at Chaffee. Most of their trade goods be loot from little towns and travelers."

"Did the Chaffee market always want what they had to trade?"

"They muddled through with coal and chalk beer, but now and then the market wanted somethin' different. Window glass did real good, and ammunition and guns. Sacks of food be the best, but wood furniture, books, clothing, lumber, steel tools and horses from time to time sold well.

"The bigger clans kept a spy in places where trade be good. Brady be like that."

"Albedo," Pete said. "While we be talkin' ask the

armory drone to bring a dozen loaded 9mm clips to the motor pool. We need for him to reload the jeep's machine gun and put in a rocket launcher or two.

"Pete," Albedo said. "The armory drone is collecting your weaponry. I ran a level one diagnostic of the damage done inside the shelter by the explosion. All the utilities are intact. May I inquire about your destination and expected return time?"

"Albedo, Matt and I be goin' to shoot up the Chastain's hangout. Then we be after the old man. It won't take long.

"Oh, Albedo, have the drones see what needs fixin' in the livin area and get some help for the women to lift the panels."

"Yes, Pete, the drones will get started right now."

Pete and Matt sat at in the kitchen ready to eat. Their morning meal would have to hold them all day if they had to run-down the old man.

"Is the Chastain camp close to Chaffee?" Matt asked.

"Their camp be about half way between here and Chaffee," Pete said. "Chaffee be a good place for the old man to go. After the little towns be leveled the bandits started in on the travelers. Even my great grandpa Morgan was in on some of that. He be changed when he be offered a prison to run. My great grandma Pat went to tradin' the leftovers sent to the prison by the wall cities folks."

"Brady made a remark that the Chaffee market wasn't what it used to be." Matt said. "I wonder if that's why he was so far east. What happens if the trader's stop coming?"

"My fathers told me that Chaffee would eventually dry up, and when it did it be leavin' desperate people in the desert, and desperate people do desperate things.

"Throwin' explosives instead of shooting, now that be desperate.

"I could take care of the women, and there be a few still here, I got food, water, medicine, and I could see they got a start in a town like Nash City. Do you know what I'd get in return? They'd drag some poor fools back to their caves, and in fifteen years I'd have to kill 'em all over again. And, what's so strange the young ones would hate me worse than the old ones. If I leave the women alone they will probably curl up in some empty corner, all alone, and die."

The conversation had ended and several minutes later Matt was first to speak.

"When do you want to go after the old guy and his brood of little devils."

"Ain't no rush. I know how to get across the river bottom east of the Chastain camp. I'll need a little light. The old man won't be there until later on tomorrow, so after shootin' up his place we'll look for his trail goin' cross country. We'll find him on our way back home."

"Why do we need to shoot up his place?"

"I gotta do somethin' after what they did to us. It tells 'em we be strong, and we don't take any crap off of 'em. If I failed to do this they would think we be weak. They may actually respect strength although I ain't sure they respect anything."

After the jeep was far enough away from the shelter Pete turned on the lights and turned up the speed. Matt thought they were vulnerable because of the noise of the motor and the lights. He was told not to worry.

"What're we doing at the old man's camp if he ain't there?" Matt said.

"I'm gonna point out a thing or two," Pete said. "Then we'll stop long enough to light 'em up. After we finish with their camp we locate the Elder."

By the time Pete had enough light to cross over the edge of the riverbank, Matt was able to see the countryside.

The surface of the land ahead of them was flat with an occasional rugged hill or rocky outcropping poking out of the ground. Dead white skeleton trees filled in the view to the east. Early morning light exposed two or three narrow rows of plants in the shade of a steep south side.

"Green corn rows," Matt said. "I'm surprised."

Chapter 9

Pete stopped the jeep atop a hill and spent several minutes scanning the countryside looking for signs of life through his binoculars. Matt was forming an impression of the landscape.

Scars in the soil told Matt that Chastain buildings were once a major part of a farm community. He identified concrete foundations, long fence lines crested by weeds and blow dirt, and rusty farm machinery ever so slowly melting into the ground.

Matt blamed wind for much of the destruction. Half covered scattered irrigation pipes, a windmill toppled into a rusted stock tank, and piles of lumber that once stood against the wind. The time of people had slipped by, but like weeds they would come back if the rains returned.

Pete saw movements.

"I see the Chastains be here. Some of the little kids be outside to play. Look around the yards and you can see what they got to play with."

"I was having the same thought," Matt said. "Is that a church off by the skeleton trees?"

"Yeah, it be a Baptist Church. This be what I wanted you to see."

Pete pulled the jeep closer to the church.

"It ain't in the best shape, but it be better kept than most desert buildings. When the wind blows you can hear the bell in the steeple from way off. In the back you can see small crosses by piles of clay. They be new graves."

"Now there's something sad," Matt said. "Out front I see a tricycle hangin' by a rope from a branch of a dead tree. No front wheel."

"It's time," Pete said, as he climbed into the back of the jeep.

Pete loaded a new belt into the big gun on a rack above Matt's head as Matt drove slowly toward the Chastain's half-buried buildings. Little kids ran for the house as the jeep rolled into view, and Pete gave them a minute to get inside below the berm.

When Pete thought the time was right he pointed his machine gun and pressed the trigger. He put four belts of ammo through his machine gun and almost cut the buildings in half.

After Pete's message was delivered Matt kept the jeep rolling out the west side of the farm. The roads had long since been obliterated and going was rough. After thirty minutes Pete directed Matt to stop on a hill top. Elevation allowed Pete to survey the country in front of them.

Pete spoke after a second stop.

"I ain't seein' nothin' movin' out on the desert. If they be camped out, we got 'em!"

Matt pulled down his binoculars.

"Take a look out on the plain to the left. I see a white bump a long way out."

"You found something, Matt," Pete said. "I can't make it out from here. Let's go see what it is."

Pete stood as they closed in on the unknown object.

"It be a Chastain Elder. Drummonds must of got him. Keep the jeep back until I see what the signs be sayin'."

Pete looked back at Matt.

"Someone chased the old man to where he fell. He be dead or close to it when he hit the ground. Three women and one man came runnin' in from behind and stuck him. The same four left to the south when their work be done. Considerin' the distance he had to run and the temperature of the clay under the body, it happened about four hours back. Matt, they didn't leave a trail to follow. Do you think someone be watchin' what happened at our place yesterday?"

"We can check it out when we get back. The sun's gonna be too hot for me by the time we get the old guy in the ground."

By the time Pete and Matt returned to the shelter the steel panels had been retracted into the ceiling. Before Pete could do anything else, he had to inspect the part of the elevator shaft that opened into the interior of the project center. He found the base of the shaft splayed out but intact.

At the dinner table Pete was thinking about ways to close the upper part of the elevator.

"Matt, have you ever done any cement work?"

"I remember the Old Man talking about it," Matt said. "We didn't have such as that to work with. We used wet clay and straw to make bricks, and we used wet clay as mortar between flat rocks to make barn walls."

"One of the rooms in the motor pool has maybe fifty or sixty bags of somethin' called Ready Mix," Pete said. I ain't never had reason to read the small print on the bags, but I got an idea we can make concrete out of what's inside. If we can fill in the top of the elevator with cement so it could never be mistaken as an entrance, and if we stopped the word from gettin' out that the Chastains got a foot in our door, I think we be okay."

"I think we're okay if we find who it was that got the Elder," Matt said. "We should start with the truck. It seems to draw a lot of attention. You could look around for tracks while I get the horses takin' care of."

"Albedo."

"Yes, Pete."

"Put the drones to sleep and wake Matt and me about an hour before sun rise."

"Pete, this will be an ideal time to recharge batteries for the drones. Your directions are noted."

When the shelter's lights were turned off at bedtime, chemical lights came on automatically. At best chemical light was barely enough to keep Matt from walking into walls on his way to the bathroom. Jane and Bobbie had to take it for granted that shadowy corners and dark hallways were empty. Muffled conversations quickly ended in the bedrooms, and words gave way to soft steady breathing of sleep.

Two hours passed then a slight rustling sound came from behind the elevator doors. Silently the doors were wedged apart creating a narrow gap. Two darkly clad figures squeezed through the gap and melted into the shadows. Creeping from shadow to shadow they made no sound and their presence was barely noticeable. The intruders followed sounds of sleep into the hallway leading to the living quarters. They paused at the first door and listened, but the sounds were not quite right.

One of the prowlers turned and whispered.

"Woman inside, we come back later after men be dead."

The next door offered the sleeping sounds of two people. One was the big stranger.

"Big man ain't to play with," the second intruder whispered, "after what he did at truck. We cut him first and fast, don't even wake up. Woman next."

"Haze be in next room with he wife," the prowler whispered. "He feels safe in his cave, and he be sleepin' hard with full belly and satisfied woman. We get big man then Haze, and save two women for later."

A doorknob turned slowly and soundlessly. The big fellow was snoring as trespassers slipped inside. The killers were careful with every step, and razor sharp knives were held ready to strike. They pushed boots and clothing out of their way with their feet as they approached the bed.

The prowlers understood the plan of attack without saying a word. They could tell by the sounds that the big stranger was on their side of the bed and he was on his back. The woman was on her stomach on the other side. They stopped once more to listen. The person on the right would hit Matt's throat hard and fast, and the one on the left would push his blade into his belly just below the ribs then turn the knife up into the heart and lungs. They would silence their victim with a hand over the mouth.

With weapons raised the young Chastains were ready.

Swish, swish. The attack was all over. The lights blinked on as Matt and Bobbie sat up in bed bleary-eyed and troubled by the commotion.

Pete, dressed in black, was dragging the two Chastains out the door.

"I found two more Chastains. They be hidin' in the elevator when I shook at the elevator doors last night. I knew they be inside I could smell 'em. I be thinkin' I could take 'em before they got this far into the living quarters."

"How did they keep the doors closed?" Matt asked.

"I'll find out in the morning," Pete said. "I'm guessin' they wedged 'em closed with spikes."

Bobbie was clutching at her covers.

"Are they both dead?"

"Yes," Pete said.

"If you knew they were in the elevator, why didn't we go after them last night?" Matt asked.

"I wasn't sure how many there be," Pete said. "The dead woman interrupted my lookin', and I be too tired to chase someone down out in the desert. I'll keep 'em in the motor pool tonight. Tomorrow we'll drop 'em off in the pit with the rest of their family."

The next morning Matt expected to find four horses in the trailer parked by his truck. When he and Pete got to the overpass they found the horses gone. The food and

Matt's little stash of coins were gone. Half the drinking water was missing and the cupboards and drawers had been searched.

"Who did this?" Matt asked. "Drummonds!"

"Four people ran down the Elder and four horses be gone. They be one and the same and they ain't gonna hide the horse tracks. I'll be trackin' while you call Jane and put things in order. Tell her not to expect us until late tonight or tomorrow."

"Jane," Matt said, "someone ran off with our horses and about everything that was in the truck. Pete and I are gonna follow the tracks, so don't expect us until we get there, over."

"Matt, was it the Chastains? Over."

"Pete thinks it's the people that got the old man, and that would make it one man and three women, over."

"Will we be able to go on to the west coast? Over."

"I think Pete could get us ready to make the trip. He might even want to go along, over."

"Bobbie wants to know if we could make it back to the Blacktower's farm if things don't work out here, over."

"It ain't something to worry about, out."

By the time Matt finished the call and put the truck straight Pete was out of sight to the south. The trail was clear and he was running. Matt grabbed a few supplies and followed after Pete.

Pete was running full stride when the jeep caught up. After Pete jumped into the jeep he told Matt to call Jane.

"Ask Jane if she looked at the night tapes."

Matt relayed Jane's message.

"Jane said she didn't see anything around the truck until about midnight. The infra-red camera picked up two or three goin' under the overpass, it was a long way off. She couldn't tell much about any of them. None of the other cameras picked up a picture of them."

"It makes you wonder," Pete said. "Did they know where the cameras be?"

"Where do you think they're going?" Matt asked. "Are they Drummonds?"

"They be headed a little southwest," Pete said. "If they belong to the Drummond clan they need to turn east. The Drummond's hideout be about a day-and-a-half to the southeast if you was to run it. They be movin' fast so they might try to curl back around to hit us from behind."

"Do they know we are following them?" Matt asked.

"Yeah, they know."

"Why don't we turn it around on them instead?"

"The Drummonds be kind'a like the Chastains," Pete said. "It's hard to get near 'em without bein' seen. It would help if we knew which trail they be on. It be a while since I visited the Drummond camp, let's take a look."

After fifteen minutes of driving Matt turned onto a smooth blacktop road and his speed picked up.

"The Drummond cave will come into sight before noon cover-up if you be able to keep the jeep on the road."

Matt was getting comfortable with his new driving skills when Pete directed him to slow down and turn off the blacktop onto an obscure path. Matt followed the path to the top of a table rock and stopped.

"Tell me what you see," Pete said.

"Well, I don't see anything," Matt said. "Below us the land slopes down to a dry creek bed. I don't see dead trees or bushes or anything."

"You know you be in Drummond territory if the countryside be stripped bare. They gathered up everything that would burn in a cook fire. You don't see this at the Chastain camp because they burn coal.

"Drummond's canyon be on the far side of the creek bed and road. Put the binoculars on the mouth of the canyon across the way and look for trails goin' in and out."

"I see what you mean."

Pete frowned.

"I see something different. Give me the glasses a minute. The canyon be long with a big cave at the end. I'm seein' somethin' blowing in the wind on the flat above the cave. Take us on over there and we'll have a look."

Matt took a turn with the binoculars.

"I've seen something like this before. The Chinese hung up some of their victims on trees or posts. We think those things are warnings to scare people away. The things over there are big enough to be people but they don't look right. They had me strung up like that once then Jane came along and saved me."

"How did they capture you?"

"I was riding hard to get to Jane when I hit a rope stretched across the road. The next thing I knew someone was helping me and it turned out to be Jane. She killed four Chinese soldiers in the process."

"Your luck be your family," Pete said, seriously. "Did the warning signs work?"

"Yeah, some of the folks were pacifists and their church wouldn't allow them to fight so they tried to run. We saw where some of them ran right into trouble on the highway."

"I be ready to go when you be ready," Pete said.

Matt caught Pete unaware when he fired up the jeep and drove it over the front edge of the table rock. Except for a thin sandstone top layer the incline was well within the jeep's limitations. Matt picked up speed rapidly and he found it necessary to dodge a few boulders.

Matt tried to talk as he bounced across a washout.

"I didn't mean to surprise you but I thought I could see a way down that wasn't too steep and it feels like cover up is close. Going around might have taken too long."

Matt drove into the mouth of the canyon shortly after darting over the edge of the flat top.

"Go on to the back of the canyon as far as you can go," Pete said. "Wait in the cave out of the sun, but keep an eye on the mouth of the canyon until I get back. I be takin' a quick look at the top of the cliff."

Pete returned to the cave moments later.

"You be right. I saw four Drummond women and one man hung on steel posts, and they be up-side-down. I think they be already dead when fires be set under their heads. They be up there a long time."

Pete pulled a raggedy old tarp out of a cave corner and threw it over the jeep.

"The Drummonds ain't gonna mind if we cover up in their cave. I think the last of this clan be up above us."

Matt reached under the tarp and brought out a jar of canned fruit before he returned to the cave.

Pete had leaned back against the cave wall and propped his carbine against his shoulder.

"That fruit will make you thirsty," Pete said.

"I got two jugs of water in the jeep, so I'm gonna have peaches. I can share or I can eat the whole thing."

"If you eat the whole jar full it'll make you sick, so I guess I need to help out."

Matt served up the peach sections with his pocketknife.

After Matt had finished eating and drinking he walked around the cave looking at its odd design. The cave entrance had been reduced in size by filling in the sides with large stones and sealing the cracks with wet clay. The tarp that covered the jeep was the winter flap that kept the north wind out.

The main chamber of the cave had man-sized notches dug into the walls. Matt thought that the compartments were for sleeping forty or fifty people. Taking into account the poorly defined trail in the canyon and the absence of a midden outside he was surprised that so many might have live here.

The back of the cave dropped twenty or thirty feet into a small shallow pond of fresh water. Matt looked at the water mark on the bank and he saw that the water level had dropped little by little over a long period of time. It was the same old story.

By early afternoon siesta time was over, and Matt was busy hooking the tarp over the front seat of the jeep expecting to keep the sun off. The radio was full of static, which stopped as soon as he pulled out on flat land.

"Jane, over."

"I'm here, Pete, over."

"All Drummonds be dead and we got new raiders

runnin' on the desert. Stay inside and keep watch on the monitors. We ain't got 'em figured out yet, out."

The southbound horse trail didn't vary in direction except for a slight jog toward a farm with one stone building still intact. Matt stayed in the jeep while Pete looked around. Minutes later Pete returned.

"I got a bad feelin' about this clan," Pete said. "They avoided our cameras and they ain't on the run. They know what we be doin' before we do it."

"Are they wanting us to follow them?" Matt asked.

"That be my guess. They be ridin' the rough and they be deliberate. We be just minutes behind 'em when they stopped to cover up.

"The people took their time eatin' and sleepin' here, and they pulled out about the same time we left the cave. They probably gonna let us get close enough to see 'em about sundown."

"We can go a lot faster than them," Matt said, "so why don't we find a better road and get on the other side of them?"

"Let me think on it. How be our fuel holdin' up?"

"I filled up yesterday and you know how far we went today. The can on the back of the jeep is full."

"We crossed a big south bound road a few miles back," Pete said. "I think it will take us close to a bridge we can use to drive over the Big Red River bed and I'm thinkin' they come from around there. We can get there before dark and it'll take them longer."

"Are we gonna ambush them?" Matt asked.

"I don't know," Pete answered, "depends on if they be friendly or not. I be suspicious about the man."

Chapter 10

After Pete located the bridge, an overland search revealed footprints of three women and one man on a north-south foot trail. The people were running.

Pete decided to run the trail to the first hill that would give him a clear view to the north. He saw dust in the air long before he spotted the horses.

"Matt," Pete said, upon his return. "Horses be kicking dust up ahead. The man probably be lookin' backwards for us. I look for him to stop shortly to spend the night lettin' us catch up. He ain't gonna like it that we didn't fall into his trap. He'll most likely be on the move well before sun up, and he'll still be lookin' over his shoulder. We might as well drive over to the other side of the bridge, if it be holdin' us, and I can set up a surprise for him on the other side."

The horses and raiders were hanging their heads as they passed by Pete squatting in the shadows. The early morning sun was bright and everyone was squinting as they crossed the bridge. The jeep was well out of sight and Matt was able to watch over Pete and the raiders without being seen. The man and his three women would have continued on if Pete hadn't called to them.

"Hey old man, keep your movements simple. We got guns pointed at you and I don't know how steady my shooters be. You would have whipped me for makin' the mistakes you be makin'."

The man lifted the brim of his floppy old hat. Matt could see the black patch over his left eye, and he thought he caught a hint of recognition in Pete's voice.

"Matt, this is one of my fathers, calls himself Patch."

"Pete," Patch said, "I saw where you took yourself some outsiders. Your women handled theirselves pretty good against Chastain's kids. Son, you need to understand one thing, you be here because that's where I wanted you. Makes no difference if you got here first. Your brother got a gun on your friend . . . has had all morning. He be twice the desert fighter you be. He wouldn't never allow anyone to get the drop on him."

Pete thought a minute before he responded.

"First of all there ain't no one with the drop on Matt, I personally checked all the vantage points, and what be more I don't have a brother. I got you and your women covered and you can't call it a stalemate because that be one you will lose. It be odd that you claim to have a desert fighter in the Patch clan. If there be actually someone out there and he learned his skills from you he didn't learn much."

Patch hated bein' bested by anyone.

"I'm gonna have the kid fire a warnin' shot."

The signal was given, the shot was fired, and a bullet

struck a glancing blow off the hood of the jeep and went whining off into the distance.

"You're shootin' warnin' shots now," Pete said. "I recall you makin' a point that there ain't no such thing as a warnin' shot. I don't think your shooter has a clear shot. The only thing he can see be the front of the jeep. Matt, did you see where the shot came from?"

"Yes," Matt answered.

"Why don't you give him something to think about?"

Matt stepped in front of the jeep, lifted his M-1 and empties an eight-round clip at the puff of smoke that hung in the quiet morning air about one-hundred-fifty yards to the west. The sounds of running followed the last shot.

Patch couldn't hide his anger as he swore under his breath and struck his leg twice with his fist. As fast as his anger exploded his attitude changed. The red in his face returned to the normal desert brown, the hatred in his eye softened as did the cutting edge of his words.

"I came back to your cave three times after we broke out of Chaffee but weren't no one at home."

"I spent a lot of time searchin' for my mother," Pete said.

"Ruby, she be on the red pony. She and Blade helped get me out of jail. Ruby, this be my other son, his name be Pete Haze. I done told you about him."

Ruby nodded in silence.

"Ruby, you and the girls can uncover," Patch said. "Pete be family. Pete, this be Ruby, and my daughters Stella and Ella. I call 'em twins because they look like twins but they ain't. They be years younger than you.

I'd match them against most anyone in the desert except maybe you.

"James Robert be your half brother, and he be albino so we don't allow him out in the sun at all. The sun makes him sick."

"Where be Blade off to?"

"Come over to my camp and we'll talk over a jug and some food, but first tell me about this man behind you, and who are the people of the big truck?"

"They be the people who own the horses that you be ridin' and the food you be eatin'. Matt, come over and meet one of my fathers."

Patch tilted his head ever so slightly.

"I'm pleased to meet one so wealthy as yourself. What we borrowed can't be of much importance to one that has so much."

Matt played along in order to help maintain Patch's perception of Pete as a desert clan leader.

"You are welcome to the food. We have always shared what we have with those less fortunate. As for the horses, we don't know who they belong to. I think you would call them borrowed. They are as much yours as ours."

"Matt be the brother of my wife," Pete said.

Patch had already started the horses along the footpath as he spoke.

"It be good that he be family so we don't have to quibble about ownership."

"Will we need to find cover before we get to your camp," Pete said.

"We be about fifteen minutes on," Patch said. "Once we get off this foot path we can go a lot faster."

Patch's camp wasn't what Pete expected. Most desert people lived underground because of the intensity of noon heat. The Patch clan lived in low-slung tents covered with a hodgepodge of burlap, woven rags, tarpaulins, and plastic. The tent cover was firmly anchored with cable and the bottom edge of the cover was rolled up a foot or two when the wind wasn't blowing. The tents were backed into thorn bush scrub on the east side of two large bluffs.

The best thing the Patch clan had going for themselves was a windmill and concrete tank that stood about sixty yards down an incline to the riverbed. Pete wondered if the windmill was ever turned off because overflow from the tank supported a growth of grass and weeds. A few tracks in the mud indicated that wild cattle were taking advantage of the water and grass. Matt and Pete were invited to taste the water, and after they bragged on the quality they were given permission to use as much as they needed.

Patch ushered Pete and Matt into a large central tent where they sat cross-legged on a big rug in the center. Ruby and the girls fixed a meal over a fire in one of the smaller tents.

"Looks like we gonna be movin' before winter comes," Patch said. "We been here longer than anyone else that lived in these tents."

"You plan on leavin' fresh water," Pete said. "You got enemies over here?"

"No enemies," Patch answered. "We got no more close fuel for night fires this winter and the animals is gettin' into our gardens."

"You can use the horses to range out a long way to get your fuel," Matt said. "If you can locate a wagon you can

JOE ALLEN

get a lot of flat wood from old farm and town buildings like everyone else does."

Presently Ruby brought in a big kettle holding a stew-like concoction and she placed the kettle on a flat rock in easy reach of the three men. Ruby had three tin plates and two cups so Patch and his company dipped their meal out of the kettle onto the plates. The rest of the family had to wait.

Ruby had no eating utensils so Pete and Matt had to learn new eating skills. Pete watched Patch without actually looking at him. Patch moved his food to the edge of the plate and scooped it into his mouth with his fingers.

Ruby seldom spoke except to her children, and she had good reason to be quiet.

"I'm sorry we don't have plates for . . . "

Patch interrupted her.

"Woman, we don't have to apologize for anything. Bring me one of the rum jugs from the other room."

Ruby closed her mouth and hurried off. As she passed the stew kettle she grabbed the cup used to dip stew onto the tin plates. The cup had to be wiped clean before the grog went in. Ruby offered the cup to Pete but Patch stopped her.

"Men don't need cups, Ruby."

Pete's first big gulp from the jug took his breath away and he found it difficult to speak. The shelter had liquor but this was the first time he did more than sniff the bottle. Pete wondered why people deliberately drank such wretched swill.

The albino sat behind Patch and he made Matt

82

nervous. It wasn't the lack of pigment, it was the intensity of his stare. He gawked at Pete like a cat watching a mouse. Now and then James Robert failed to blink for a noticeable length of time.

Slowly Matt became aware of the sisters interest in him. A glance in their direction brought on the hint of a smile behind those dirty little faces, and they eventually looked down, which Matt took to be a sign of respect.

When Ruby was sure that everyone was finished she moved the kettle and the girls to another tent where they did whatever women do while men pass the jug.

Once more Pete asked about his other father.

"What happened to Blade?"

"It be a long story," Patch said. "It started the second time your ma and me and Blade went to trade day after your grandpa Kyle burned down half the town. The Haze clan had a way of makin' folks uneasy. After the man healed up he went off east huntin' Chastains and their friends. People changed their names because he be so persistent.

"Me and Blade was in a tavern drinkin' beer when I saw this sullen lookin' young woman in the back of the room. She beckoned to me to come over to where she be seated, but the barkeep told me she stuck a knife into two other guys that tried to drag her into the back room. I went over to her and asked why she cut up the other guys, and she said that they choose her but she didn't chose them. Then she said I chose you. It made sense to me. Her name be Ruby.

"Little by little I learned that Ruby was taken from her parents by Drummonds during a raid down on the gulf coast. She be too young for a man when they picked her up and when she be old enough she wasn't havin' any goin's on with a Drummond. The old women beat her and burned her. Almost killed her. After a while she was traded to a beer brewer in Chaffee. He lost her in a poker game. The gambler traded her in for his bar bill. I was the only one she would not stick her knife into.

"The next year when we went to Chaffee to trade, Ruby tells me I got a son and he ain't got no color to him. I told her he couldn't be mine because I had you and you had color to your eyes and hair. She said she wasn't with no other man so it had to be mine.

"Sorry, your ma, saw to it that I gave money to Ruby and the boy to live on. Sorry couldn't stand the thought of a woman selling herself to buy food. Your ma was tougher than whang leather but she was as good hearted as I ever came across.

"Then one day we go into Chaffee and the judges boys got warrants for Blade and me from up north. They toss us in jail and Sorry goes a little crazy. She finds Ruby and gives her a gun to slip to us. Some of the guards gets shot up, all the prisoners are set free. Ruby, the albino, and me and Blade head for the desert."

"Why didn't you come back to Haze Territory?" Pete asked.

"We had to ditch the other prisoners to keep 'em from followin' us back to the shelter, and then we ran out of food and water. Me and Blade stopped at the shelter two or three times but we couldn't get anyone to let us in. The judge's thugs had our keys locked in the safe at the jail, and you don't just open a window and crawl in the shelter. Blade saw you in your jeep once, but you be just a kid and you be goin' the other direction.

"Needed a place with food and water so we went south. In the long run it be best because none of us was a Haze and you and your ma was. We didn't want to drag another woman in there and have to report that we lost our keys. We would have to rely on your ma to let us in and she was actin' strange. Blade thought it be best to move on.

"Down south in bayou country Blade got us in with a group callin' theirselves the Afro Clan. We stayed with them for two years and we be doin' fine until a big guy told 'em to get rid of the whites. It be okay for Blade to stay because he be dark enough but we had to go. Blade got buggered-up protectin' us.

"Too bad you didn't find my grandma's friends in the south," Pete said, "he be a black trader that traded with us."

"After I left Blade I be kind'a at loose ends. I played a lot of poker and drank a lot, and I even went on a killin' spree and got even for Blade. But, it be Ruby that straightened me out. Someone told us about this place and we liked it here.

"I been thinkin' about what Matt said about draggin' in wood and I decided I might see if it'll work."

Patch took a long drink of rum before he continued.

"Whatever happened to your ma?"

"I think the Chastain women found her dead up north," Pete said. "She wondered off into the desert and died. The Chastain Elder that you killed told me about her a few hours before you got him."

"Do you know why I went after him?" Patch said.

"Tell me," Pete said.

"The judge's goons told Blade and me that the Elder

was the one that got word up north, and they should come and get us. I didn't know where he be until you started shootin' at him. He moved pretty good for an old guy."

"Did you put the Drummond women up high on steel posts as a sign to me?" Pete asked.

"No," Patch said. "That be for Ruby. All the Drummond men left for Chaffee so we hit their cave and took their women to the top of hill to punish them for what they did to Ruby. She's been a different woman."

"How did you get by in the big wind storm that hit a while back?" Pete asked.

"Ruby and the girls be here by theirselves, and they say they had to shut down the windmill. Blew a lot of dirt around but the tents took it okay. Me and Jim Bob be rootin' around in a ghost town west of here. We saw a building literally explode in the wind. Wasn't as bad here."

"Is there anything south of here?" Matt asked.

"Ain't nothing to the southwest," Patch said. "It was all reduce to rubble years ago. Ain't so much as a ripple in the ground for as far as the eye can see. We got some big ruins maybe five days walkin' southeast. One thing or another brought 'em down."

"What about some of the closer places to the north?" Matt said. "That ghost town you mentioned could give you a lot of fire wood that could be stacked on the other side of the bridge until you needed it. You could build fences and covers for your gardens. You got lots of good water."

"Sounds mighty ambitious for someone that ain't gonna do any of the work."

"It would take a lot less work than moving to another

camp. Knowing your back trouble and all, you could supervise knocking down the buildings and loading a wagon. Your girls could handle all that and the horses."

"I'll give it some thought."

Patch talked himself into a noon nap, and soon after everyone had drifted off.

For several minutes Matt lay with his eyes closed listening for something. He suspected that hours had passed because the air in the tent had cooled considerably. Except for the squeak of the windmill fan and the splash of water he heard nothing. Matt looked left and right and saw no movement. Outside the shadows were long and the wind of mid-day had gentled some. The sound was metallic and he heard it again. Matt peeked out the tent flap and saw Jim Bob fiddling with the machine gun on the jeep.

Pete sat up rubbing his eyes.

"What was that sound?"

"You brother has his hands on the machine gun."

Pete stepped through the tent flap.

"Jim Bob, get away from the jeep!"

The albino ignored the order.

"I decided to shoot your big gun."

Matt started toward the jeep but Pete stopped him.

"Matt, let me handle it, I'm bein' challenged. Go back inside, you can't be part of it."

Matt pulled back the tent flap and ducked in. He glanced back in time to see Pete drag Jim Bob from the back of the jeep and pitch him into the dust on his belly.

"When a superior gives you an order, you obey instantly. It's one of your father's rules!"

Chapter 11

Matt positioned himself to see through the flap opening. He didn't hear Ruby enter, and he jumped a little when she handed him a cup of hot tea. Ruby stepped lightly in front of Matt's right shoulder, and she spoke in that quiet desert whisper.

"This is Patch's doing. To him it's a rooster fight, and there ain't nothing we can do but hope they don't kill one another."

"Ruby, I hope you understand," Matt said, "Pete doesn't fight for fun. If he's forced to defend himself he'll kill the kid."

"I don't know, Patch turned Jimmie into a killer just like he did Pete. Patch ain't none better his own self."

"Isn't there anything I can do?" Matt asked. "I'll fight the kid or Patch for fun if it's just a fight that he wants."

"There's a thing you can do but it ain't about the fight. The dispute was made and it'll be there until it's finished."

Matt turned toward Ruby.

"You say there's something I can do?"

"Yes, for me and my girls. They ain't got a problem with a hard life. They'll do just fine anywhere, and they can hold their own against any raiders, but we had a time or two when I thought we couldn't make it. I tried to get Patch to take us back to the underground shelter where his other son lived, but he wouldn't go back. He said it made a person soft and soft people die in the desert.

"The girls are of an age now and it's all I can do to keep Patch and the boy off of 'em. All I need is a passel of slow-minded babies bumpin' into things. If I bring the girls up to you will you take 'em in and see to it that they get decent men to stay with. They would be happy to go as breeder girls as long as they don't get whipped too much. They ain't the prettiest but they're a long way from ugly and they're good workers. They been taught to fight by Patch."

"What about you, Ruby?"

"I'll be stayin' with Patch. He and the boy needs someone to do for 'em. They won't bother you about the girls because I got final say about some things, and they both got scars to prove it. The girls gave me their word that they'll mind your decisions about them if you were to be their guardian."

Matt hesitated.

"I have a wife and a sister, the girls would have to fit in with them. But, they are family and of course they are welcome to my protection."

Ruby looked contented.

"I'll bring them when the time is right."

Don't wait too long," Matt said. "We are on our way to the west coast. You have about a week or so before we're gone."

Ruby nodded her head and appeared to be in deep thought.

Out in the dust Jim Bob's sullen impudence was gone as was Pete's heavy-handedness. Shirts were off and knives were pulled.

"I can see where they both got their training," Matt said.

"Both of 'em gonna need stitched up," Ruby said, with no emotion in her voice.

Matt had misjudged the albino. The boy had a heavy frame with good muscle mass. He was quick on his feet and he was aggressive. Jim Bob put two nicks in Pete before Pete made his first move.

Pete was so engrossed in studying the moves of the white one that he hardly noticed the blood. For several minutes the fight amounted to thrust and parry, advance and retreat. It could have been two wild animals looking for a weakness.

Matt smiled as he watched Jim Bob. He saw a bit of a twinkle in those pink little eyes, and the albino's tongue came lolling out between his teeth just before he rushed. Pete circled away from the blade held low in the albino's right hand. *The albino thinks Pete is running from him when Pete ducks away from his right hand,* Matt thought. *That'll cost him because Pete's faster.*

The white one charged in low wildly swinging his knife at Pete's legs, but his attack was undisciplined. Pete easily spun over Jim Bob putting a long cut down his back. They both rolled to their feet and charged each catching a wrist in their free hand. Pushing and shoving got them nowhere.

As time passed early energy faded and the combatants,

now almost too tired to stand, glared at each other, shoulders drooping, arms hanging, cuts and scratches stinging from sweat.

Pete turned as if to walk away, but after his second step, all in one move, he bent over with legs spread and launched his knife from below. He aimed at the spot where Jim Bob's belly should be. The albino's knife went sailing harmlessly over Pete's back. Pete turned to find the albino falling to his knees holding his left hand. Blood was seeping out between his fingers. Pete's knife stuck all the way through Jim Bob's wrist and hand. The fight was over.

Pete picked up his shirt and pulled free his knife.

"I hope this puts an end to it. If you lose the use of your hand blame Patch. I know he put you up to taggin' me for a knife fight. The next time I'll just shoot you."

Matt and Pete were cruising along up on the flatland when Pete reached for the radio.

"Hello back there. Anybody be listening?"

"Hello, yourself. Your voice is so clear you must be close to home. Is everything okay?"

"We be runnin' out of gas. If you think you can drive the other jeep it be ready to go. Load up some fuel cans and drive 'em out to us."

"I can do that," Jane said. "How am I gonna find you in the dark?

"Go south on the big highway. Be careful on the bridges and watch for our headlights. If you miss us I'll fire three shots, so listen. Oh yeah, bring some antiseptic and gauze."

"What happened?" Jane asked.

"I got into a knife fight with my albino brother," Pete answered.

"Really, what happened?"

"I'll tell you later."

Matt and Pete spent the next day eating and sleeping. The need for sleep quickly turned into a need to fill their time. The horses were gone, so Matt was free to work on his father's old steam truck.

Pete followed his dogs around Midwest City making rounds that were becoming less and less important. The clans were no longer a threat and Pete's mind wandered. *Patch didn't much care for the fallout shelter,* Pete thought. *He made it clear he didn't want to live here. At most he might want a handout once in a while, and that be okay.*

Except for Jane, shelter life had turned boring for Pete. Jane wasn't used to having him around so much and she often found him irresistible at the strangest times.

Bobbie was busy with musical tapes, and Matt had developed an interest in flight and the mechanics of small airplanes. Jane and Rona Ti were looking into the medical center. Everyone had questions for Albedo and the drones.

Matt asked Pete to spend more and more time in the motor pool tinkering with the Piper Apache and the Cessna. Pete understood how Albedo and the motor pool drone had helped Kyle and his cousins. Matt thought, *why not airplanes?*

"Matt," Pete said, "I understand that we be on our way west before long. I got two things I want done before we go. We gotta close the shelter and make the elevator shaft safe, and I understand Ruby wants to bring the girls to live with us.

"I know you be interested in those airplanes so if there be time I might want to see what that's like."

"We can do that," Matt answered. "Me and Jane ain't in a hurry. You were what she left home for. I know she wants to learn medicine and she can do a lot of that here. I think she'll be satisfied wherever you are."

"I be startin' on the elevator tomorrow mornin'," Pete said. "I think your truck will make an easy job of it."

"I'm thinkin' it'll take two days to get ready to use the truck," Matt said. "You and me will have to get the sacks of Ready Mix carried up. We gotta build a ramp to get the truck close enough, and we gotta mix the concrete and funnel it into the house. There ain't much of that the girls can help with."

During the cooler hours Matt and Pete dug a dirt ramp close to the opening above the elevator shaft. By the second day loads of wet concrete and rock were pushed into the shaft. When they were finished the broken down elevator shaft was a solid column of debris. After the damaged roof was pulled over the shaft and bolted into place the old house could no longer be considered a weakness.

"The old house looks like it should," Pete said, standing in the center of the motor pool. "It be time for us to work on those." He pointed at the airplanes.

"It might take a while to git 'em up and running," Matt said.

Chapter 12

Pete and Matt huffed and puffed, pulled and pushed, and eventually moved two airplanes into the open side of the motor pool. Day after day they identified parts according to diagrams in their books. With the help of the motor pool drone, engines were disassembled, cleaned, analyzed, tested and reassembled. Old age required substitution of crumbling or brittle components, and occasionally Matt had to rebuild a part in the motor pool shop. In due course the engines started and the control mechanisms worked. With Albedo's guidance they learned about maintenance, about takeoff and landing, and lastly they learned about wind and weather.

Pete used a relatively smooth street to practice maneuvering his plane on the ground. At times he hit flight speed to get the feel of the machine in and out of wind and he wanted to listen to the sounds of the motor. When Matt was satisfied that the mechanics of the plane were ready Pete was satisfied. From now on nothing would substitute for flying.

"I ain't gonna get any better until I get up in the air," Pete said, "and you tell me you think the airplane is ready so let's get it over with."

"From what I can tell," Matt said, "both planes are ready to take up. I'm gonna wait for you to come back down and tell me about it before I take the other plane up."

Pete's first attempt at flight started well. He was off the ground gaining altitude as smoothly as he expected. As Pete flew over his territory he was amazed at how far he could see. He made several low passes over the others watching from the ground.

Pete's first landing approach was started too far down the road and he bounced high a number of times and eventually he had to throttle up and try again. In all he had to make three attempts to get it right. Pete's first flight lasted about twenty minutes. Matt stayed up for two hours and he made a smooth landing the first try. Their biggest problem was learning to control flight in a crosswind.

The women would not allow the little airplanes to be put away until they had a ride. Someday Jane would have her turn flying, and she would do it alone. Bobbie was satisfied to ride with the men, and Rona Ti was happy to get her feet back on the ground.

A year had passed and the little planes were in the air as often as wind allowed. They flew over the Chastain camp one evening and observed no activity. The other camps were the same. People in Chaffee came out to see what was making the noise. Pete's airplane was the first that any of the traders had ever seen.

One afternoon they buzzed Patch's camp and decided to land after Ruby came out signaling that she needed help. The top of the bluff on the south side of the tents was long enough and flat enough to handle a landing.

"Patch ain't well," Ruby said, "and the girls be watchin' Jim Bob. His hand and wrist healed but it just hangs there, and he can't lift nothing with it. The boy tried to bend it back to normal and yesterday it swelled up like it be poisoned. I don't know if the hand can be saved."

"My sister is the best I know of at doctoring," Matt said. "We can fly him to our camp in an hour or two, and I know she will do her best for him."

Matt and Pete carried the Albino to the top of the bluff and stuffed him into the back of the airplane. They were in the air in no time and Ruby watched as they flew out of sight.

Jane had no idea what to do for Jim Bob, but she was excited about being asked to help. With the assistance of the medical drone she was able to save Jim Bob's hand. Jane noticed that severed tendons and ligaments were beyond her ability to correct. Jim Bob would be unable to lift his fingers.

While injured tissue healed, Jane worked on a way to support and protect Jim Bob's hand. With Matt's help, Jane made a spring-loaded brace to support his wrist.

Jane was feeling rather proud of her efforts as she watched the airplane lift off the ground and turn south returning Jim Bob to his mother.

Bobbie walked up beside Jane and draped an arm around her shoulders.

"Well doc, I think you need to read up on another medical problem."

"Like what?" Jane said.

"I think you're gonna be an Auntie next spring."

Jane hugged Bobbie and laughed.

"Delivering babies isn't one I have to read up on. I've been helping babies get born since I was twelve years old. How far along are you?"

"I'm late for the first time ever, and I just have a feeling."

"Have you told Matt?"

"No, I want to be sure."

When Matt returned from Patch's camp he had Stella and Ella with him. They were wide-eyed and nervous about flying, but they quickly adapted to the great new adventure. The fallout shelter was another story. It wasn't difficult to see Patch's influence on the girls' reaction. They didn't understand the shelter and they didn't like being underground.

Matt gave the girls new clothing and he took them to all the different parts of the shelter, but he spent little time telling them how to use the shiny new fixtures that were so foreign to them. His instructions were simple.

"You can have anything you want, and you can do anything you want to do."

Matt thought it was strange that the sisters elected to wear their tattered old desert clothes. He failed to realize that they didn't understand their new clothing, so how could they understand the rest of this place.

For two days they followed him around like lost little

puppies and he thought that it was because they liked the motor pool and guns.

Eventually Stella and Ella found an ally in Rona Ti. She not only had time for them, she took their education as her personal responsibility.

She told a story with the introduction to each room, and she had them practice with any apparatus that they would be expected to use. As much as they admired Matt, the girls soon lost interest in his work at the motor pool and they looked to Rona Ti for everything.

After a few days in the shelter Jane became aware that Pete ignored his sisters. If the girls came into the motor pool he soon found a reason to be elsewhere. If they wanted to ride along in the jeep he never had enough room. If they wanted to learn about a gun he had Matt help them.

Rona Ti overheard the girls talking and she felt helpless when asked why Pete didn't like them. He was their brother, he was the leader of their clan, and he didn't consider them worthy of his attention. It wasn't because they were outsiders. Rona Ti's own case proved that. She was an outsider that belonged to a different race, and yet her acceptance was never in question.

Rona Ti decided to ask Jane.

"Jane, what is problem between Pete and sisters?"

"I noticed that he ignores them most of the time, but he ignores everyone when he's studying on something. I know that I demand a lot of his time, and he and Matt are trying to get ready for our trip to the West Coast. We need to understand that Pete lived alone for nearly half of his life, and I'm sure he had to make a big adjustment when we came to live with him. He needs to know they are loyal."

"Signals of loyalty not made good for Pete? Maybe loyalty. We work on this tomorrow."

Many days went by and life in the shelter became routine. Except for Pete, the occupants failed to realize that they had witnessed the end of a way of life that had flourished for nearly four hundred years.

The desert clans be gone, Pete thought. *The killers, and the thieves, be gone. The energy needed for clans to survive caused by hate, and vengeance, and that be gone. Someday we might even be considered heroes.*

Haze clan be different.

Chapter 13

The time had come to close down the shelter and see what life was like on the West Coast. Pete and Matt didn't trust old fuel maps from shelter files, so fuel barrels would have to be stationed along the way.

"If all goes well Fort Defiance Shelter should be our first stop. I took a trip there and it be a shelter like here. It be located south of the Four Corners area on the Colorado Plateau. According to the computer there, Fort Defiance has a good gasoline supply."

"It looks like we got one stop west out of Fort Defiance," Matt said. "I think one or maybe two stashes of gasoline will get us across the Cactus Desert."

"Matt, I can't tell you much about Fort Defiance. The insides is half in the wall of a canyon and half in a dam in front of a small lake. I only spent one night there.

"The Atomic Battery be workin' and the water in the pipes be dirty but it cleans up if you let it run. Except for being a lot smaller it be organized like Tinker Shelter.

"There be People in the area so be watchful."

Early one morning Matt loaded Bobby into his airplane. Pete was already in the air and Jane followed a little later in a jeep loaded with young women.

Pete and Matt landed on the flat surface of a small mesa in the middle of what appeared to be rocky deserted country.

"We be quite a ways north of the big highway," Pete said. "The trail down below be what I followed to get to the shelter. It be a leftover of the access road to the lake behind the water dam. We have to use it to get in and out of the shelter by jeep. We need to be sure there ain't no one watching us when we open up the front door of the shelter."

To Matt, the first obvious difference between Tinker and Fort Defiance was the midday air temperature. Heat was moderate and the sky was back to its normal blue color. While scanning the area Matt was first to point out volcanic activity far to the south.

"We got smoke in the air and I can hear some rumbling in that direction. Probably too far away to be a problem."

By late afternoon clouds had drifted into view. Sunlight behind developing showers provided contrast for raindrops that never hit the ground. As the clouds grew darker a curtain of rain hid the sun and lightning followed by its thunderous eruption lent atmosphere to the opening of the watchtower by Pete and his clan.

Pete took a moment to watch the rain splatter on the window.

"It be worth the trip over here just to see rain."

Pete waited until rain surrounded the tower before he

opened the trapdoor in the floor. As the trapdoor slid out of the way a flight of stairs came into view. At the bottom of the stairs a light switch was turned on and the floor panel above closed. Pete used another key and code to open the door into the center of the shelter.

A breathy rather sexy female voice spoke to the intruders.

"Please state your name and rank."

"Pete Haze and family," Pete answered.

"Pete, I remember, you complained about my water."

"That be me right enough. I forgot your name."

"I am Luna. If you want me to use a different name and voice I will be happy to make changes. Please have your family members check in at the computer desk."

"You need to turn on the electric, water, and climate control. Do you have drones?"

"Pete, I have three drones one each for the kitchen, medical office, and motor pool. We are smaller than Albedo's shelter."

Bobbie hurried off to the tactical to turn on the surveillance cameras and the radio. As the lights blinked on she saw an inch wide crack in the ceiling. She followed the crack down the wall across the floor and on to the wall on the far side of the room.

"Luna, tell Pete to git over here as fast as he can!"

"Bobbie," Luna said. "Pete has acknowledged."

Pete rushed into the tactical.

"What be the problem?"

"Pete, you need to look at the big crack in the wall. It may have opened one of the containment areas."

Pete looked surprised.

"This be new. Had to happen slow because it didn't bring down the partitions. The big battery in utility be first thing we need to see about. Luna, give me a run down on the condition of the whole shelter."

"Pete," Luna said. "The atomic battery is safe. Water and gasoline storage levels are normal. The crack missed the kitchen and medical areas. Sleeping rooms and motor pool are damaged. The map room and safe may have the most damage."

Pete breathed a sigh of relief.

"It looks like we be able to stay. We be lucky. This reminds me, I need to show you the backdoor."

Pete used the wall map in utility.

"Here be the escape door. It leads to a tunnel that drops down to a ledge above the reservoir overflow canal. Luna opens and closes a valve in the lake to control water level. Everything must be holding or she would tell me. Bobbie, if I forget to show the others be sure to show this map."

Bobbie returned to tactical and switched on the radio.

"Jane, are you listening?"

"I'm here," Jane replied. "How did the trip go?"

"We spent a lot of time checking out the area before we went into the shelter. And then I found a big crack clear across tactical. Pete thought it may have gone through the battery but Luna said it missed anything vital."

"Who is Luna?"

"Luna is like Albedo but with a woman's voice."

"Why did you wait so long to call me?" Jane asked.

"We had a little thunderstorm go through about the

time we opened the shelter, and after that I thought I should wait until Pete checked out the crack." "Did the partitions come down?" Jane asked.

"No," Bobbie replied, "Pete thought it happened very slowly. As far as we know it's probably still happening. How is everything with you people?"

"Rona Ti and the girls found some music tapes and they're about to drive me nuts. They call it 'rock 'n roll' and they play it so loud. I finally had to turn it off."

"I'm going to sign off now. I'll see you about sunup."

Pete and Matt were in no rush moving gasoline out on the road. They often took time to work on an airplane. Some of the engine parts were not trustworthy. In the evenings, before sundown, they explored the surrounding territory. They referred to their little trips as 'testing repairs'.

Matt was hoping to find a farmer or rancher to visit.

"Pete, we can find out a lot from farmers. They'll probably know something about the West Coast. All they need to know is that we're friendly and just passing through."

One evening a return flight put them over a wagon trail coming off the highway. The trail crossed over a ridge and continued on to a high country cabin just below timberline. The cabin had smoke coming from the chimney, and several people came out to wave as they flew over three or four times. *It would take the better part of a full day to get there by jeep,* Matt thought.

Chapter 14

As usual, Pete was skeptical of strangers.

"I don't think we have to worry about the people up here the way we had to at Tinker," Matt said. "I'll talk to them if you'd rather stay out of it. This is the kind of thing we had to do to get work back home, so I'm used to talking to strangers. I'll even work for them for a few days if I have to. Bobbie and Jane can go along with me. Bobbie's pretty good at wheedling information out of people, and Jane can talk canning, and sewing, and doctoring for hours."

"It be best that you people do the talkin' to new people," Pete said. "I ain't got much tact with strangers. While you're in talking, I'm going to stand by the radio until I know for sure what the people are like."

The jeep was overheating some as Matt, Bobbie, and Jane pulled up in front of the log cabin. A middle-aged woman in a plaid shirt and an old, denim skirt came out to greet them. Her blond hair was pulled back and knotted, and her ruddy complexion told Bobbie that she was used to working outside. Six youngsters piled out the door behind her and she made no attempt to keep them from converging on Matt and the jeep.

The lady's soft blue eyes twinkled as she held out her arms to Bobbie and Jane.

"I've been watching for you people ever since you flew over us yesterday. It was near impossible to hold class today. The children kept asking if I thought the people in the airplane would come see us. I told them not to get their hopes up because they might not come back. We don't have a good place for them to land their flying machine."

The hugging went on and on as Matt sat in the jeep watching.

"You're going to have to excuse me and the children for being so excited. You people are the first company we've ever had up here. For that matter we haven't had anyone outside of the family at the ranch down below. What am I going to call you dear people? Oh, I'm so flustered I didn't tell you who I am. My name is Cleo."

"I'm Bobbie, she is Jane, and that's my husband Matt in the jeep."

"It's a long ride up here from the highway. I'll bet you are bushed."

"It was a nice ride except for the jeep heating up," Bobbie said. "Are you and the kids here all alone?"

"My goodness no, Ard and two of the boys have three flocks of sheep up in the alpine meadows. Two older boys and two of their cousins are out in the Cactus Desert trying to put together a herd of mustangs. Two of my older kids and their families are doing all the farming down below. My teenage girls are watching the house and keeping my flowers watered. I bring the younger ones up here for schooling in the summer because it's cool and there's less distraction."

"Then here we come and disturb your class."

"We've been reading, writing, and doing numbers all summer, and to tell you the truth the kids were holding up better than me. Besides, there isn't a soul here that would miss a chance to be with company, and that includes the ones that don't even know you're here."

Cleo looked over her shoulder.

"Jonah, take a pony up to the meadows and tell your father that we have company. The boys can put the flocks together and they can take turns coming down to visit. Tell your father to bring along one of the yearling rams."

"Cleo, please don't go to any trouble for us, we can't stay long."

"I know that nice people tell you that, but I am going to go to as much trouble as I possibly can, and I'm going to drag you right along with me," Cleo winked at Bobbie. "You are my excuse to have a party and my family just loves it when we do something out of the ordinary. You might just as well plan on spending some time with us because we're not going to get it all said tonight. I've been busting at the seams to make a fuss over something and now I've got you."

"I want you to know that we didn't come empty handed," Bobbie said, happy that she had planned ahead. "I packed a few boxes full of things for you when I found out we were coming to visit. I hope I picked the right things."

JOE ALLEN

Bobbie beckoned to Matt to bring in one of the box from the back of the jeep.

Cleo looked at the content of the box with great surprise and wonder.

"Where on earth did you get new clothing, and food, and wine, and all of these other things? Everything looks so new. The clothes haven't even been worn!"

"Oh, we found them and as it turned out we had more than we could use. I'll bring some more things for the others the next time we come by."

Cleo quietly gave directions to several of the children and each moved quickly to do what was asked.

"I want you to know that we would do it up right if we were at the ranch, but we are going to do pretty darn good right here. Now, I don't know about you but I'm going to cook and talk your ears off, and I'm going to love every minute of it," Cleo paused and put on a false frown. "You had better have some good stories to tell, because we haven't heard anything new since the last baby learned to talk."

"Well," Bobbie said, mysteriously. "There might be a thing or two we could tell you, but if you want the whole story we should get the others up here."

Cleo was caught by surprise.

"You mean there are more besides you?"

"Yes," Bobbie said. "Pete is in the Cessna waiting for a radio call, and Jane and three girls are back at our camp. We came here from Tinker."

Cleo was more serious.

"Is that Tinker Prison?"

"It was at one time," Bobbie said. "The prison's been

closed for a long time, in fact what was left of it blew away in a wind storm just a few weeks back."

"Wasn't it dangerous crossing the Red Clay Desert?"

"Yes," Bobbie said. "Until we met up with Pete. He taught us what we had to know to live there, and once a person knows his limitations it's not such a bad place.

"Pete married Matt's sister and he's very protective of us. Oh, by the way do you think that Pete could land his airplane on the trail if we moved some of the larger rocks?"

"I don't know why not. Let's get Matt and the older boys on it right away. Matt will know if it's good enough won't he?"

"He should," Bobbie said.

Cleo wanted to get back to the young women.

"How old are these girls back at your camp and are they spoken for?"

"Three are teenagers and they're not spoken for. Why do you ask?"

The smile was back on Cleo's face.

"We have two boys that are talking about girls, if you know what I mean. And, there aren't any girls around that don't belong to our family. Are your girls old enough to be interested in boys."

"All I can tell you is that we can get them together and see what happens," Bobbie said. "Pete is responsible for his sisters and he probably would be sympathetic to such a meeting."

"Do you realize the possibilities?" Cleo asked. "You and your family could come down to the ranch and stay with us possibly for the whole winter."

"That's something we would have to talk about,"

Bobbie said. "We are on our way to see the Pacific Ocean, and we don't know anything about the Cactus Desert or how things are on the West Coast."

Cleo looked at Bobbie knowingly.

"Well, we can talk about both places, but you won't find any place better than our little valley. I know that you have to see for yourself, and it will be a good trip for you. You'll see things out there that you won't ever forget, and there are places where you have to be very careful.

"It'll be an advantage if you can take your flying machine because there are so many places that you can't even get to by horse anymore."

"I think we should get you to help us make plans."

Cleo was remembering the past.

"It'll be fun for Ard and me to bring up some old memories of when we were young. We moved away when we were just kids. People told us not to go out on the Red Clay Desert. I guess you could say that we got trapped into staying here, but you won't hear either of us complain. From what I have heard, I think we were lucky. Some of our friends and relatives took a more northerly path and most of them made it, but it wasn't easy.

"I was expecting our first child and winter wasn't far off so we stayed behind. It turned out to be what we were looking for. Some of the children here are nephews and nieces that came back to live with us because they didn't like it where they were."

"I'm going to call Pete," Bobbie said. "He needs to be on his way and he needs to bring the rest of our group."

Pete was leaning against one of the wing struts when the ground started to shake. It was almost undetectable at first, then came a couple of hard jolts that knocked him off his feet. Pete looked back toward the shelter. He saw Jane and the girls running toward the airplane. Dust and smoke emerged from a narrow crevasse that appeared to be in line with the shelter.

A sense of urgency filled Pete's mind as he rushed to the open motor pool door.

If I gotta cave-in goin' on I gotta save as much as I can before that battery pops.

Once inside, Pete found the air saturated with dust, and he had several new cracks to investigate. Pete was surprised that the safety partitions had not dropped out of the ceiling. *They must be wedged in place.* The big crack in Tactical had slipped another two inches and part of the ceiling near the east wall was crumbling onto the electronic equipment.

"Luna," Pete yelled. "You still working?"

"Pete, I am in a state of disrepair, I will soon be forced to shut down." Luna's voice had changed and it was full of static. "I am unable to . . . do diagnostics of shelter environment, and I have lost contact with . . . my drones."

"Luna, I got two questions. Is the water holding in the reservoir, and is the atomic battery okay?"

"Pete, I . . . do not . . . goodbye Pete." Luna's voice ended in a static growl.

The damage found during Pete's quick examination was a crack in the wall and ceiling of cold storage. Pete was sure the frozen food would be lost. The motor pool appeared to be the only place that had no new damage.

The quaking seemed to be over so Pete returned to his airplane to use the radio.

"Matt, this be Pete."

"Hello Pete," Matt answered. "Where are you calling from, your signal is weak?"

"I'm calling from the Cessna on the ground," Pete answered. "How fast can you get back here?"

"It'll take a while just to make the turn off. Is there a problem?"

"Yes! We had a quake and there be damage in the shelter. The motor pool be okay, no leaks that I could see, except for cold storage. We may lose the frozen food. If we get another quake we be losin' the whole thing.

"I'm going to see what can be saved and me and the girls will start moving it into the motor pool."

"Pete, leave on your radio. We felt a little shake here but it wasn't bad. Do you want us to bring help?"

"Can you trust them?" Pete asked.

Bobbie came out to the jeep in time to hear the end of the conversation.

"Tell Pete I trust them," Bobbie said.

"Bobbie says they're good people. She trusts them."

"Then bring everyone," Pete ordered. "We might as well clean the place out. We can't stay in here. I'm not sure it won't cave in! You'll understand when you see it."

It was well past midnight when Matt and Bobbie pulled in with Cleo and two of the older boys riding in the back.

"Lots more help will come from the ranch after the sheep are locked up," Cleo said. "Ard has horses and wagons, and he can bring the whole family."

"If we move out in a jeep with its trailer loaded right now can we be at your ranch before your men leaves?"

"I'm sure you can," Cleo said.

"We got one Jeep and two trailers loaded with dry food, clothes, kitchen tools, and furniture. Jane and Bobbie will drive as soon as the jeep be gassed up and the trailer hooked up."

Cleo studied Pete as he gave directions and put everyone to work. "You have to be Pete. I'm Cleo, what do you want us to do with these things?" Cleo asked.

"Do what you want." Pete wasn't in the mood to talk, "it's yours. Me and Matt be flyin' frozen food and medicine back to Tinker. Move as much as you can into the motor pool until your other people get here."

"Why are you doing this for us?"

"I don't like waste," Pete said.

Days passed and stripping of the damaged shelter was near completion. When a second earthquake hit, Pete was helping Ard and his sons pull the wiring and pipes out of the utility pod while Matt filled the two airplanes with fuel. Matt held onto an airplane wing, but the men inside the shelter were helpless as they bounced off the walls.

This time the partitions came plummeting out of their slots in the ceiling. Some came so fast that they were jolted out of their tracks.

Pete was sure that tactical, medical, living, and office quarters were lost. Walls continued shaking and water gushed into the utility pod where he had been working.

Lights went out, sparks flew, and Pete could smell smoke from an electrical fire. In a matter of seconds the emergency lights came on and he spotted a big fracture in the wall and ceiling above atomic battery containment.

"We've got to get out of here now!" Pete shouted, "Follow me!"

The door in the back of the utility pod was locked. Pete fumbled with his keys momentarily. *What be the code?*

Water was up to Pete's knees and the others were pushing him from behind. Finally, he turned the handle and the door burst open. The rush of water behind Pete knocked him down.

The whole group was carried by fast moving current down to the catwalk and on toward the overflow channel that came from the reservoir.

Pete managed to catch hold of a railing long enough to stop the others. The overflow valve must have been damaged because the roar of the water just below them was so loud that they could hardly hear.

Pete yelled at the top of his voice.

"Don't be afraid of the water!" Pete yelled. "Hold your breath and dive deep. You'll be out the other end in two seconds."

Panic was on the face of one of the younger boys, "I can't swim!"

Pete thought, *that makes two of us,* but he yelled, "You got no choice, this place is about to blow! Grab the back of my belt, and don't let go for anything!"

Pete dove into the water pulling the reluctant little boy behind him. Seconds later they shot to the surface in the center of the pond that was quickly forming below the dam. Momentum carried Pete into shallow water. When he could stand he had trouble getting the trembling little boy to turn loose of his belt. In short order the others surfaced in the pond behind Pete.

"This way," Pete yelled. "Let's get out of here! This place is coming apart! Ard, were any of the others inside when the partitions came down?"

"The other man was working in the motor pool, but I think the rest left with the last load of gasoline which was to go to the ranch."

"I'll check out the motor pool," Pete said. "The rest of you go to the airplane."

The third set of shock waves hit as Pete left the motor pool. The ground was rolling under his feet as he ran toward the others waiting by the plane, and he was knocked to the ground more than once.

"Matt be gone! Everybody, in the plane!"

Chapter 15

The airplane was barely off the ground when a loud whomp caused all of them to turn and look back. Pete circled the reservoir once to see what was happening below. Water gushed out through a big fissure in the dam and the shelter had caved in on the side of the hill.

Conversation was at a minimum on the way to the ranch. *Ain't no need to talk about it*, Pete thought. *Atomic battery or gasoline storage probably popped.*

For the next couple of days Matt and Pete slept and worked making ready airplane fuel while Cleo and Ard marveled at all that had made up the interior of the shelter. Now it was their property and imagination would be needed.

"Look at all that gold and silver, Ard," Cleo said. "What on earth are we gonna do with that."

On the afternoon of the second day, two of Cleo's sons rode into the yard and announced that a herd of about thirty mixed mustangs was in a sheep holding pen about a mile up the valley. They could use some help.

It was then that Cleo altered their plans.

"I'm sorry but tomorrow we are going to have a party. We have company and I plan on eating, and dancing, and singing until I'm are too tired to stand up. Then we are going to tell stories, and believe me you don't want to miss the stories that these people have to tell."

This party would be remembered for years to come. Cleo was the type of person that saved things for special occasions, and this was what she had in mind. She had cherished recipes in her family that had been passed on from generation to generation dating back to the Old Country. For Cleo, the excitement was being in the kitchen with the other women sharing these little secrets and putting everything together so that it was all ready at the same time. The men didn't have to say a word. Watching them stuff themselves was enough.

In the evening Cleo and her daughters tuned-up their piano, violin, and banjo and strummed away through a series of polkas and fast moving dance music. Everyone danced except Pete and his sisters. Dancing wasn't a tradition in their background. They didn't know how to dance and they were too embarrassed to admit it. Jane wanted to dance with Pete and she asked him once, but she knew better than to push, so she danced with Ard while Cleo played the piano.

Pete looked at the faces of those on the dance floor and he looked at the faces of Stella and Ella. When the music stopped Pete took Ella by the hand and led her up to one of the unattached young men. He lifted the young man's hand placing her hand in his, "Can you teach her?"

The young man nodded.

Pete looked at Ella.

"Learn."

Pete returned to where Stella was seated, and he reached for her hand. As she stood three of the other eligible young men hurried over to Pete's side. The eldest of the three muscled his way in front of the others.

"Sir, I'd be honored."

Pete placed her hand in his and returned to his chair.

Pete was feeling rather pleased with himself when the boy that he helped out of the shelter sat down in the chair next to his.

"You didn't know how to swim when we jumped into the water did you?"

"I knew how to float," Pete said, looking at the boy.

"Were you afraid?" the boy asked.

"Yes," Pete answered, "but not because I couldn't swim. I was afraid the place was going to blow up with us inside."

"I was afraid of the water," the boy said. "It was going so fast."

"That's why I made you hold on."

"You can't dance either can you?"

If he had been a man Pete would have given him a look that would have backed him off, but he was a boy.

"When I was young, there were other things more important than dancing."

The boy nodded his head knowingly and left. A few minutes later one of the boy's older sisters came over to Pete and asked if she could teach him to dance the polka. Pete was about to reject the offer when his young friend interrupted, "My mother said that a man can't refuse to dance with an unmarried girl. It's a rule. Pete, there ain't nothing to be afraid of. This ain't fast moving water I'm talkin' about here."

In the privacy of the kitchen it took about five minutes for the young lady to pass on her moves to Pete. He had precious little rhythm in his soul, but the steps were simple and in short order she led Pete out on the dance floor with the others. It was a small price to pay for the disguise of domestication which was so important to Jane. He knew deep down that he would never completely lose the feeling that came with living alone for so many years, and now he was able to swing his pretty little wife around and around in step with the music.

Eventually the dancers tired and Cleo asked that they all gather outside by a big fire that Ard had been tending. The mountain air was crisp at night and the fire felt good. Cleo supplied blankets for everyone to put around their shoulders and some were lucky enough to have a partner to share the blanket with.

In spite of the protests, Cleo decided to skip the singing and get right to the story telling. She called on Matt first.

The Blacktower story was followed by Bobbie, then by Rona Ti, and Jane finished with the truck ride out west. She took great pleasure recalling her first meeting with a desert man recognized for his fierce reputation.

Then Pete was called to speak and the group fell silent. Most everyone had worked with Pete during the clearing of the shelter, and they remembered him as a man of few words. He gave orders, but he never spoke if he could use a gesture, and he was strong, maybe he was as strong as Matt.

Pete's new friends didn't know if they liked Pete. He wasn't friendly, yet he protected one of their family without hesitation, and he was generous. There was an air of anticipation in all the young men and it carried over to the women. Here was a real desert clan leader at their campfire. He had to fight and kill to stay alive, and he looked the part.

Pete's dark unruly hair fluttered in the breeze, and the light of the campfire seemed to accentuate the intensity of his gaze as it moved from person to person. Pete never smiled as he talked and the furrow in his eyebrows grew deeper as his story moved from his ancestors to his battles with the other clans. He could feel his own blood beginning to heat with the telling.

Pete ended his story and added a brief note.

"When we return to the desert, we will make it a good place to live. Now Stella or Ella can tell you about their part of the family."

Clan woman weren't expected to speak out in public, but Jane had done it and their leader requested it, so the girls would try. It was kind of a dirty trick they wouldn't be ready, but it was also kind of an honor to be singled out this way. Actually, Ella put together a reasonably good story.

Cleo stood when Ella had finished.

"I have so many questions, but they will have to wait. Ard and I want you to hear about things you will see on your trip.

"I came from a small Norwegian community in the Cascades, and Ard's people lived on the west edge of the Palouse hills. My people raised sheep and grew fruit trees so we did okay.

"Ard won't talk about his family so I will have to. When Ard was fifteen a group of old men, dressed in black coats and black hats, came to his farm and tried to bargain with his father for Ard's two older sisters. Of course his father refused. That night they came back for the girls, and they killed his parents and burned the farm. They chased Ard and his brother for days, and one-by-one the old men gave up and dropped out. Ard and his brother saw what was happening. They followed the drop outs, and punished them but Ard said no to killing them. The two boys ambushed the last old man still on the chase and he was killed.

"A year later Ard found his way to our village and we met for the first time We were both sixteen and that was old enough so Ard proposed. I thought I was lucky to be asked even though he wouldn't tell me his name. He never did tell me his real name.

"The Cascades had several quiet old volcanoes, but when three of them started smoking several young families formed up a work group going south, possibly as far as the San Joaquin Valley. We all joined the work crew and Ard and me had been married less then three days. Some of the women even talked about a caravan going east. We said maybe.

"A man told us that four generations of his people stayed in big coastal cities. They made a living by salvaging things that people left behind when the roads broke down. People literally walked out carrying their possibles on their backs.

"A person can find small pockets of people here and there all over that part of the country if the water is good and farmland is clean and not shaking. Except for a few folks that want to be left alone, they are friendly people. You will probably have to go north of the redwoods to find beaches that are safe. The western edge is kind of crumbly so don't go into the water unless it's used by local people."

"All-in-all, we think we were lucky to find our little valley in the mountains. Our winters are cold and we get several feet of snow each year. We're always ready for the snow and skiing is how we have fun. Lots of elk in the high country and we eat elk when we get tired of mutton. If the winters are real bad we will have wolves trying to get into the sheep barns, and during the summers we have to watch out for bear."

Jane was curious about neighbors.

"Do you have neighbors that you trade with?"

"No one close," Cleo said. "Every other year we trade with people from way down south. They make iron tools like mower blades and hay rake teeth that they know we need and they help us put up hay. Their women make a very nice cotton cloth that we like, and they will fill wagons with pine knots, post and fencing lumber, and firewood. This will get them two wagon loads of sheep."

By the time all the talking was finished most of the listeners were fast asleep by the fire. Ard put another log on the fire and settled down by Cleo. He pushed the last of the tobacco into his pipe and lit it with an ember from the fire.

"I hope they bring tobacco this year," Ard blew out a large puff of smoke as he spoke.

Cleo yawned.

"It's almost dawn, I should start up a fire in the stove

and get a pot of coffee on. The kids and our company will be wanting their breakfast soon."

"Why don't you sleep a little yourself. If anyone gets hungry your daughters will take care of them."

"The boys wanted to get started on their horses early," Cleo said, and she yawned once more.

"The boys may have altered their plans you know," Ard said. "There are other things to think about."

"Such as?" Cleo asked.

"Did you forget about the girls that just happen to be the right age for two of your sons," Ard said.

"The boys couldn't take their eyes off them, could they? Do you think that Pete will agree to let them go as mates for our sons?"

"I agree to let them choose their mates as all of us have done," Pete said.

Ard and Cleo were taken by surprise by Pete's quiet words from behind them.

"Oh, Pete you startled me," Cleo said, peeking over Ard's shoulder. "Would you let them live here with us?"

Pete didn't answer right away, but when he did his words were not what Cleo expected.

"Your family be a lot like Jane's family. I like that. If the young ones choose each other they can live where they please, here or at Tinker Shelter."

"The boys will be so happy." Cleo yawned again and went to sleep.

The next morning Pete told the girls to ride with him to the north pen where the horses were being held. The rest of the men and boys were already there.

Pete spoke first.

"Can either of you tell if Ard's sons be interested in you as a mate?"

Ella looked down.

"They like us. Do you want us to take a mate from their family?"

"Last night I told Ard and Cleo that it was up to you and the boys. If you take your mate from their family, I will take their family into our clan and open the doors of Tinker Shelter to them. Be sure they understand"

Stella looked at Ella.

"Pete has accepted us in his clan," Stella whispered.

The girls understood the honor that Pete was giving them, even if the others would not. They knew of none higher in the extremely private lives of clan people. They both touched Pete lightly on the arm.

"Talk to the young men as soon as we get there. Give me a signal when your agreements are arranged. We will have Matt and Jane listen to your vows, and they will enter your names in Jane's Bible. On this, her way is better than ours. Do you know about babies and being a wife?"

"Ruby told us," they said, in unison

"Can you be ready by this evening?" Pete asked.

"Yes."

Chapter 16

Pete swung up to the top rail of the fence by Matt.

"Did you get everything worked out with the girls?" Matt said.

"I'll know in a minute," Pete answered.

Stella and Ella watched the boys taking turns being thrown from feisty little mustangs. Boys laughed and chided as brothers often do when they're showing off, but the girls noticed only two of them.

The girls had worked to the side of the young man of her choice. After whispers were exchanged, a glance and nod told Pete what he wanted to know.

Pete, Stella and Ella were first to return to the ranch house. Simultaneously they become aware of the lack of activity and the absence of sounds. The jeeps had flat tires and a puff of smoke came from an open shed door.

Two strange horses had been tied to a post on the far side of the house, and two scruffy looking men lay face down in the dirt behind the horses.

Bobbie staggered out of the front door. As she spoke

she tugged at ropes that were hanging from her neck and shoulder.

"Men from down south rode in and took two of Cleo's daughters and Rona Ti! They said something about offerings to God!"

"Where is Jane?" Pete asked!

Bobbie was a little breathless but she pointed south.

Pete understood and sent a silent signaled to Stella and Ella.

"Ten men wanted to water horses like always," Bobbie gasped. "Cleo recognized several of the men. She called them by name! When the leader found out that our men were gone, they pulled guns on us!

"They started ransacking the house! Cleo and Jane jumped one of the men! Cleo got cracked on the head with a gun barrel, but Jane got to Pete's quiet gun! She dropped one of them in the house, and she may have hit others out front.

"I don't know what possessed her to go running after them on foot!"

Bobbie stopped to catch her breath.

"The leader was tall and very skinny. He had blue eyes that were kind of wild looking and his nose looked like an eagle beak. He wore a white collar, like a priest, and he continually babbled orders!"

Bobbie was holding a clean tea towel to the bloody place on Cleo's head as Ard walked in the door. Cleo was still unconscious.

Speaking quietly, Bobbie looked up at Ard.

"They were the men that come here to trade for sheep. Ard, they have two of your daughters."

Ard's face turned red.

"Why have they done this to us? We have always treated them well! We always gave more than we got from them! Boys, you'll need guns!"

The sun had gone down and the house was getting dark.

Matt had the old army rifle strapped to his back, and he waited patiently by the screen door. Out side two small figures, dressed in black, darted across the porch and jumped on the backs of their horses. Something stirred outside the door. It was Pete, and Matt could barely make out his words,

"Matt, keep the others here. I be doin' what has to be done and they won't! We won't come back without the girls!"

Matt was going to protest being left behind, but he heard the horses rushing off into the shadows.

Pete and his sisters were held back by the darkness, so they were well beyond the big highway by the time they caught up with Jane.

Pete lifted Jane to the back of his horse. She was near exhaustion.

"You okay?" Pete asked.

Jane answered as they exchanged weapons.

"I'm okay, but they took Rona Ti! How is Cleo?"

"She'll live," Pete said. "Did they hurt the girls?"

"Not yet. They know they're being followed."

"Why didn't you take a horse?"

"Once they got away from the ranch house, they stopped. I thought I might get close enough to get shots at them. Then they ran for a while and then they stopped, and I'd catch up. I got four of 'em with your gun."

"I counted three dead," Pete said.

"They had one man try to ambush me, but I got him back in the rocks. When it occurred to me that they were going to out run me, I was too far away to go back. I knew you'd be coming."

"Your clothes be too light," Pete said. "You'll have to stay with the horses."

At sunrise Pete was still following a warm trail. Riding out of a dry wash onto a wide, empty plain, Pete came across the bodies of two men. He found no blood on the ground under the bodies.

"They probably be dead in the saddle. I think you shot six," Pete said, scanning the southern horizon. "It looks to me like the Priest wants to be across the open country before we see where he went. He ain't hidin' nothin'. Look across the valley his dust still be in the air behind him."

Pete was about to charge off across the valley when suddenly he pulled up his horse.

"I know where they be going," Pete declared.

The others waited for Pete to continue, but he changed directions. Across the emptiness and up the grade they came to a trickle-water stream dribbling into a rocky pool.

"I'm going to water the animals," Pete said. "We can rest the horses before they have to carry us over the ridge to the south. There be a town on the other side."

"How do you know there's a town there?" Jane said.

"Saw it from our plane. Sleep for a few minutes if you can. There be a stream bed to follow on the other side."

"Do you think he might try to trap us?" Jane asked.

"Can't say, I don't know these people."

By late afternoon Pete peered over the top of the ridge. A volcano stood like a giant tombstone at the other end of the valley. Today the monster was quiet but Pete could see a cold, black lava flow extending away from a large fissure. Bit-by-bit lava was claiming farmland that must have supported the town.

Jane was happy to tend the horses as Pete and his sisters inched their way through cedars, junipers, and sage. They dodged cactus and boulders all the way down to the edge of town.

Most of the buildings were a dirty, gray stucco with faded, red tile roofs. Pete saw neither people nor animals. The town was quiet. Not so much as a barking dog broke the silence.

Stella and Ella stood at the end of Main Street and they pointed at a large, white mission. Several horses stood at a rail near the front door.

Pete's quiet observations were interrupted by singing, but he couldn't make out the words. It was more like chanting, and it was coming from the mission.

"The kidnapped girls," Pete thought, *"has something to do with the mission."*

Stella and Ella watched exits while Pete approached the mission from the shadows at the rear of the building. A gentle push at the bottom of a basement window allowed him to pry open the latch.

The chanting continued from above as Pete slipped through the window. A short hallway led to a spiral staircase that ended in an empty dark choir loft above the front door.

Pete was watching from the shadows of the empty loft when the chanting stopped and the congregation dropped to their knees. A man in black took his position behind the pulpit. Pete scanned the room as the Padre called for silent prayer, but the girls weren't present. He saw no children at all, and only a few women.

Pete concentrated on the Padre. He saw a man that was tall and slender, just as Cleo had described him. He appeared to be in his late forties. The Priest's eyes were deep set and his lips were thin and pressed tightly together which pulled the corners of his mouth down into a permanent grimace. However all features were diminished by a truly magnificent nose.

Chapter 17

In a strong, clear voice the Padre began his message.

"I have told you repeatedly that we are in a life and death struggle with the forces of evil. More and more of our cropland is lost each day, and you heard me tell you that one day evil will be at the very door of God's house. This is what I believed.

"I have always believed that sacrifices were the source of our protection because they were individual acts of love for God, but they must be offered without absentmindedness. You can't be thinking about dinner during a prayer or while you are making offerings.

"Praise Him because you want to, not because I say that you should. Psalms 54:6,7 verifies this, 'I will freely sacrifice unto thee: I will praise thy name, O LORD; for it is good.'

"Then, I began to see a different picture, Zephaniah 1:3 told me, 'I will consume man and beast; I will consume the fowls of the heaven, and the fishes of the sea.' I say we did what was expected of us. "But something was wrong. Our offerings must have been incomplete.

"It's all there for us to figure out. God tells us in Acts 7:42, 'have ye offered to me slain beasts and sacrifices by the space of forty years in the wilderness.' The LORD recognized our offerings. Did we withhold something that God wanted, when God, himself, withheld nothing from us, not even His son, Ephesians 5:2. Christ loved us enough to offer himself as a sacrifice to God.

"Then we sacrificed our own children. But wait, Psalms 54:37 tells me we were doing the right thing for the wrong reason. 'Yea, they sacrificed their sons and daughters unto devils.' The monster at the other end of our valley is not the devil's creation. It has to be God's creation, and evil is in my ignorance not seeing this. Our sacrifices should have been for the volcano, thus for God's creation. I was surely blinded by the devil so as not to see this.

"Follow along now and it will be as clear to you as it is to me.

"Zephaniah knew and he tells us the whole story beginning with Chapter 1, Verse 7, 'for the day of the LORD is at hand: for the LORD hath prepared a sacrifice, And it shall come to pass in the day of the LORD'S sacrifice that I will punish the princes, and the King's children, and all such as are clothed with strange apparel.'

"People we live in King's Valley, we are the King's children, and speaking of strange apparel, those foreign girls were wearing trousers like those of a man. What sort of blasphemy is this?

"And, who amongst us can forget, 'a great crashing from the hills,' it was on the day the monster was born. 'That day is a day of wrath, a day of wasteness and desolation, a day of darkness and gloominess, a day of clouds and thick darkness.'

'And I will bring distress upon men, that they shall walk like blind men, because they have sinned against the LORD: and their blood shall be poured out as dust, and their flesh as the dung.'

'Neither their silver nor their gold shall be able to deliver them in the day of the LORD'S wrath; but the whole land shall be devoured by fire of his jealousy: for he shall make even a speedy riddance of all them that dwell in the land.'

"Does any of this ring a bell? The volcano is God's wrath, and I in my foolishness, have been witnessing against it. This was my false prophecy and I must pay for my error.

The true prophecy is being fulfilled. Our blood is as dust on the ground and the flesh of our children is as the dung rotting on the black rocks.

"How do we know what to do? Romans 12:1 tells us `that ye present your bodies as a living sacrifice, holy, and acceptable unto God.' This, undoubtedly, is for me. And that which follows is for the young women that wait His judgment

"When is the time? Amos 4:4 `bring a sacrifice every morning.' What should not be sacrificed? Proverbs 15:8

`The sacrifice of the wicked is an abomination to the LORD.' Deuteronomy 15:21 `And if there be any blemish therein, as if it be lame, or blind, or have any ill blemish, thou shalt not sacrifice it unto the LORD thy God.'

"Our next sacrifice will be perfect. They are fair of skin, young, strong, and unblemished, and they be unknown to man. They are perfect.

"How shall we prepare the sacrifice? Mark 9:49 'every sacrifice shall be salted with salt.' Philippians 4:18 'an odour of a sweet smell, makes a sacrifice acceptable, and well pleasing to God.' Psalms 118:27 'bind the sacrifice with cords, even unto the horns of the alter.'

"You see, the Bible gives us directions.

"So, what shall we do? Exodus 5:17 'let us go and do sacrifice to the Lord.' Will it be enough? Hebrews 10:12

'But this man, after he had offered one sacrifice for all his sins, sat down on the right hand of God.'

"And what of tomorrow? First Samuel 9:12,13 puts it this way, 'for there is a sacrifice of the people today in the high place,' and 'he doth bless the sacrifice.'

"Also from First Samuel 9:9 'for he that is now called Prophet was beforetime called Seer.' People, the Good Book recognizes me. My father told me that I would be able to see things in the Bible that others couldn't see, and it was up to me to follow through on what I saw. I was fooled once by false prophecy, but the list is long that fell into that trap. I was put on earth to light the way while we stumbled through the thick darkness 'as a blind man' for am I not Prophet John Baptist Seer, dedicated to the LORD by a sainted father on the day he sacrificed his wife, his first born, and himself to God on the first day of the LORD'S wrath forty years ago?"

Chapter 18

He be sacrificin' the girls to that volcano tomorrow morning, Pete thought, *and they need to be prepared tonight. He could be hiding them anywhere. We need to look for a high place. That be where we'll find the altar. Probably up by the lava flow. There'll be a lot of dead stuff strewn around. And, he be offerin' up himself as well.*

It took several minutes for Pete to work his way back to Stella and Ella.

"Did you see where the Priest went?"

"He left by the back door," Stella said. "He got lost in the buildings. He be on his horse, but he weren't in a hurry."

"Stella, find a horse and take it to Jane. Meet Ella and me on the far side of town. The padre be takin' our girls up to the black lava for some kind of a ritual. Be ready by sunrise."

The sun was still below the horizon for Pete and Ella, but enough light made it through early morning mist to expose pinkish clouds that were drifting down from the volcano's mouth. Pete got a whiff of the hot foul breath of the volcano, and he knew it would soon be on them. Pete led the way through layers of cold black lava, and he was not surprised to find countless bodies strewn around a flat area that held a platform topped with four altars.

Many of the remains were human.

Pete and his sisters found hiding places nearby, and they watched faithful followers of Profit Seer arriving. The assembly was aware of the volcano as it bubbled and belched out small puffs of dark smoky ash, and they saw large black birds circling high overhead.

A procession of acolytes, identified by their white robes, stopped in front of the raised platform and three small figures were pushed forward and forced to kneel. Father Seer, dressed in a red robe, stepped out of the shadows and raised his arms and called for quiet. Pete breathed a sigh of relief. *The girls be alive.*

The prisoner's white robes were pulled off, and the girls were allowed to huddle together in the cool air of morning. Except for flimsy cotton veils they had no protection from the elements.

The preacher stepped forward and blessed each of the girls to the fulfillment of her destiny, and he blessed himself with equal fervor. Thereafter, each girl was escorted to her altar, lifted up, and tied in place. The girls neither struggled, nor pleaded for help.

The preacher's robe fell to the platform and he placed himself on altar number four. He wrapped cords around the altar horns and his wrists.

The Padre's assistant had watched many such rituals, but this would be his first chance to wield the obsidian dagger. His voice quivered with excitement and cold as he gave instructions to the assistant on the platform.

Pete listened to the quiet prayers and chanting, and he wondered what they were saying. The words ran together becoming a sing-song of meaningless noise. Then it was time for the dedication of the first sacrifice.

"He be ready to kill her!" Ella whispered.

The veil was opened, and the assistant Padre counted down the ribs until he located the soft space between the fourth rib and fifth rib on the left side of the breastbone. This would be the soft spot where he would slowly push the blade. Slowly, until it cut into the wall of the heart.

As the preacher ran his fingers over the smooth skin of the rib cage he couldn't help but admire the beauty of the exposed young body stretched out before him. He was in no hurry.

The young Priest pulled the ritual obsidian dagger from a sheath in his robe and placed it length-wise on the girl's chest. The tip of the blade indicated the soft spot that he had chosen. He raised his arms, praying as he turned to face his followers.

The young man dedicated his work to the satisfaction of his God, and his voice grew stronger as his prayer continued. He turned and reached for the dagger when a figure dressed in black stepped out of the lava bed and called to the young man. *Had the lava rock became alive and was it giving orders?*

"Step back!" Pete yelled.

"No," the young Padre yelled. He was full of the spirit, and he was sure of his protection. He lunged forward as Pete jumped up to the platform.

The Priest was shot three times, but he managed to lift the obsidian dagger and bring it down on his victim. The point of the dagger broke off in the girl's breastbone. He raised his arm and turned to the next altar and he took another bullet. As the young preacher died he fell forward on Rona Ti and dragged his blade across Rona Ti's chest leaving a bloody trail.

It took a moment for the escorts in white to muster their courage and pull their knives. They rushed forward weapons raised when Stella and Ella stepped out of the lava rock.

"The lava is alive!" a follower yelled. "We're gonna die! Git out my way!"

The followers leaped back looking around for more lava to come alive.

Jane was on her way with the horses as soon as the shooting started. Pete saw her pushing her animals through the crowd toward the rocky platform. When he turned to order the release of the girls he saw that his sisters had already cut them free, and they were gathering robes to cover them.

Pete's attention turned to the fourth altar. It was empty. The Priest was gone. While Jane got the girls ready to ride, Pete checked the trail used by the Priest and his escorts, but he could find no trace of Father Seer.

Pete returned to the altar platform and spoke to the people below.

"Did others amongst you help steal the girls from the sheep herders?"

The crowd stopped, and as a unit they turned to look at three men that held back a little from the others. The crowd said nothing.

Pete understood, and he pointed his gun at the kidnappers. They turned and ran as Pete spoke.

"Be smart enough not to go back to the sheepherders. I'll be there."

Three kidnappers were almost back in town, but it wasn't difficult for the bystanders to tell when Pete caught up with them. The runners fell forward on their faces and Pete rode on.

The leader of the kidnappers had escaped, and Pete hated loose ends. He wanted to send the others on while he searched for the Padre. After all Jane could care for the kidnapped girls, however Pete's clear-cut objective from the beginning was to find the girls and take them home.

Jane was first to speak.

"Pete, I have to stop and take care of the girls wounds. One is bleeding and I think there is something stuck in her breast bone where the cut is, and Rona Ti has a cut across her chest."

"Should I go ahead for the airplane?" Pete asked.

"Let me look at the wounds first."

Chapter 19

The incident of the kidnapping was eventually put behind them. Cleo was good at redirecting people's attention. Wounds were healed, fears were reconciled, and smiles returned to the faces of the ones that had suffered. Pete was the only one that couldn't let go. It wasn't over for him as long as the Padre was out there looking at him.

Most evenings found Pete perched high on a vantage point watching over the ranch. Jane didn't understand, but she didn't question things that Pete did. Jane came to visit often and Pete welcomed her company. She would snuggle in tight, and he would put his arm around her shoulder to ward off the evening chill. She knew better than to talk because Pete needed to listen as well as watch, and if she interfered with either he would ask her to go. On an evening such as this Pete learned about the baby.

Cleo thought that the weddings would allow Pete to relax, and she included him as much as he could tolerate. He was pleased that his sisters were accepted by Cleo and Ard, and he was pleased with the young men that Stella and Ella had chosen. He had something else to think about for a while.

Cleo interrupted Pete on his way to self-imposed sentry duty.

"Pete, have you got a minute?"

Pete stopped and looked at Cleo.

Cleo was a little hesitant.

"Pete, don't take this the wrong way. We don't want you to leave, but if you folks are going to the coast you need to get your plans made or wait until next spring."

"You be right," Pete said. "I almost forgot. The girls can keep watch."

For the first time Cleo thought she understood a little of what was hidden behind those deep, dark eyes. Family or clan as he called it, was everything to Pete. To be accepted as a member in a Desert Clan wasn't a symbolic gesture. It was a promise of responsibility for which there were no words, and it was seriously given the night of the dance. Such a gift must be acknowledged.

Conditions looked good when Matt made his flyover of the traveler's highway route. Bridges appeared to be intact, the gasoline supply was okay, and the sky was clear. The plan was to be on the road in the morning.

Cleo had not been idle. She and her daughters had prepared a surprise banquet. This dinner was her very best effort because she wanted it to be remembered. Cleo had things that needed to be said. Ard had trouble expressing himself and he stuttered some when he talked in public, so the words were left for Cleo.

At the end of the meal Cleo stood and quiet followed.

"You must all wait just a moment before dessert." Cleo said, with pride. "We surely thank the Lord who has blessed us with happiness and new prosperity. And, we wish God speed to our friends that start their trip in the morning. I tried to give everyone the impression that this was a going away party, but it's a lot more.

"I mentioned that part of our blessing was happiness, and my happiness was doubled with the return of my beautiful daughters that were taken from their home and made to fear for their lives. Part of my happiness is the marriage of my handsome young sons, and part of my happiness is the surprise that came with all the various gifts from the shelter.

"Pete and his family have a lot to do with my happiness. They returned my daughters, they married my sons, and they gave us many wonderful new things.

"We will make use of materials and equipment from the shelter all the rest of our lives. But, none of this is as important as his final gift. Pete has given us his name and his family. I've thought about this a lot. Ard has never allowed us to use his last name and truthfully we haven't needed it. So, from now on, with Pete's permission, we will be known as Ard and Cleo of the Haze-Blacktower Clan."

Pete looked down and nodded his head. He was not surprised that Cleo had recognized and understood the importance of his actions. *If Cleo understands,* Pete thought, *her whole family will eventually know and understand.*

Matt and Pete decided to take Cleo's suggestion and use an airstrip named Edward located near the end of their journey. If they left one airplane at the base they could return in the other and meet the jeep at the first camp site. Regrettably a thunderous rainstorm had intensified between them.

"Looks like a lot of wind in those clouds," Pete said. "I say we go on in the morning."

Jane watched rain clouds developing to the southwest. She looked for an overpass to protect them but the old highway offered nothing that would keep her and her passengers from a drenching. Jane pulled off the road as the rain started and together they attached the canvas top and sides. For the rest of the night Jane drove in the rain, Bobbie fussed with cold food, and Rona Ti tried to sleep.

The second day, in the middle of the cactus desert, Pete and Matt sighted a series of overpasses at a major highway interchange.

"This is where we should find Jane's jeep," Matt said. "She probably pulled in under a bridge looking to keep dry."

Pete landed on the highway as Jane and the girls emerged from cover to greet them.

"Jane, I'm surprised you got this far what with the rain and all," Matt said.

"I had to drive all night in the storm," Jane said. "We were soaked putting the cover on the jeep. This place is our first stop."

Pete had been keeping an eye on several campfires under the old highway behind the girls.

"Bobbie, what be your thoughts about the people behind you?"

"They're kind of like Cleo and Ard," Bobbie said. "Jane has been visiting several cook fires where women were preparing a noon meal. They call themselves Planters and they invited us to share their meal. The women are friendly and talkative and they told me they spend their whole life wandering up and down the highway between small planting plots with good soil. They don't eat meat."

Rona Ti had listened quietly to planter conversations until she heard the name 'Young' mentioned.

"Is Young a Chinese family?" Rona Ti asked.

"Yes," the Planter said. "The Young family lives at one of the other camps. Old man Young has seniority in that group. I'll send a messenger to tell him he has a visitor from China."

The whole Young family came to listened to Rona Ti's story. Grandfather Young was unaware that the rebellious Old God-King had been driven out of China but he understood why so many infant girls left China to live with relatives in other countries.

Grandfather Young had a personal question for Rona Ti after her story was over.

"If you return to China will you be a ruler?"

"I am not meant to rule," Rona Ti answered. "However, one day my son will be God-king of China . . . it is written."

"Do you carry the God-king inside?" Grandfather Young asked

"Not yet, but I will when the time is right."

The old man smiled and looked at Pete.

Bobbie and Jane had no difficulty drawing information out of their new friends.

"Where do the planters call home?" Jane asked.

"We move from overpass to overpass," an older lady

said. "It depends on which garden is ready. Right now we have three camps puttin' out winter plots.

Rona Ti was disturbed by the scarring on the chest and abdomen of the children, and she asked about it.

"It's part of the baptism of children," a young mother said.

Whispering among the planter women ended the conversation about religion.

The next morning Matt and his women continued on in the jeep, and Pete returned to Edward to look for a place to camp.

Pete picked a collapsing Quonset hanger as a campsite. It offered the most protection from weather and it offered a place to work.

Matt will see his airplane when he gets here, so I got time to look around. I think I'll take a look at our neighbors.

Once in the air Pete was mildly surprised to see an endless expanse of weeds, sage and cactus skeletons. He saw large animals grazing below, but he couldn't tell what they were. Farm buildings here and there were still standing but they appeared to be in bad shape.

A range of mountains to the east wasn't much more than a line of dry, empty hills, and they were so eroded that he could see the gullies from where he sat. *Ain't gonna be anything to see in that direction,* Pete thought. Looking through the haze to the west he could see mountains, tall and rugged, with snow on one or two of them.

Pete flew south. He saw bodies of water slightly larger than ponds. Some of the ponds had people living by them. Individuals appeared out of nowhere to look up as he flew over.

Further on Pete made out the pointed end of a gulf with its volcanic hills and cold black lava. Broken barren low land with long cracks extended out of sight to the north. At higher elevations on his far right he came across large stands of short bushy dark green trees.

Pete continued west eventually turning north at the edge of a fog bank. He was passing over the Pacific Coastline. As the fog cleared he caught site of a huge deserted shipyard and seaport. Later, Pete remembered Jane's comment and he thought he understood. Coastal cities looked like one continuous city from north to south on both sides of the country. Pete looked for boundaries.

Inland, Pete flew over four explosion craters. They were deep and several hundred feet across and everything surrounding the blast sights had been knocked flat. It was a mystery to Pete, and he would look at it another time.

The sun was getting low in the west, and the fog bank was almost back on shore. Pete had lost track of time and he was lost. *The others will be at Edward and I ain't gonna be there*, Pete thought. *I'm gonna have to land while I got light and that means spending the night in the airplane. It shouldn't take long to find the airstrip in the morning.*

Pete had just settled into a semi comfortable position, and he was on the verge of sleep when something hit the window beside his head. Pete was immediately on the defensive. His next thought was to attack whatever was coming through the window after him.

Chapter 20

Pete came out of the airplane with his knife drawn. The old gentleman that had tapped on the window was almost bowled over when the door was thrust in his face.

They stood there for a moment looking at each other. As soon as Pete realized that the old man was no threat he returned his knife to its hiding place.

Pete was the first to speak.

"What do you want?"

The old fellow was a little shaken.

"I'm Doc Welty. I didn't mean to upset ya'. I thought ya' might be in trouble landing your flying machine in the road."

"I couldn't get back to the airstrip before dark."

"What airstrip were ya' trying for?"

"Edward."

"Kind'a out in the desert is it?"

"On the edge," Pete said.

"If ya' was in a rush I could get ya' over there tonight, but ya'd just have to turn around and come back for the airplane tomorrow."

"Mornin' be soon enough."

"There's hot coffee and sandwiches back at my campfire," Doc said. "Ma always packs a little extra in case friends stop by. Ma says that swapping stories helps the digestion, and I believe she's right."

"I didn't see your fire. How far be it?" Pete asked.

"It may be a mile or a little less."

"Get in on the other side," Pete said.

"We're goin' to fly back? It isn't that much of a walk."

"I want to keep the airplane close."

Pete sat on his heels looking into the flames. He seldom had a campfire when he was home. *An open fire can be seen for miles*, Pete thought. *Must be a safe old man's fire. He didn't get old bein' careless.*

"There's something hypnotic about a fire," Doc said. "It's constantly changing as if it's never satisfied with itself. Some men are that way."

Pete ignored Doc's remarks but he relaxed a little.

Doc nudged Pete's elbow as he held out a cup and a sandwich. The coffee was hot and fresh, and the sandwich was made with thick slices of homemade bread.

Pete paid his compliments for the coffee and food, as was his way.

"Will the fire attract your enemies?"

"Don't have enemies," Doc said. "I'm the only doctor for three hundred miles in any direction. Everyone that lives here knows me, and they're not apt to harm the one person that might be called on to save their life someday. I hope ya' like meatball sandwiches, they're my favorite and they're Ma's specialty."

Pete nodded his head while he worked on his first bite.

"What about people that don't know you?"

"Frankly, I see more airplanes than strangers, and a hooligan isn't gonna to be in an airplane. The other airplane that I see now and then belongs to the people that makes gasoline, and they give me fuel so I can make my rounds. Actually, the only people that use this road beside myself are the migratory workers, and I know them all personally. They're welcome at my fire just like you are."

"I didn't know that they still made gasoline," Pete said.

"Still a few working cars and trucks left. Most people don't drive unless they have to make time. I usually take a horse and buggy unless I'm on an emergency.

"Gasoline is something that trades well, and trade is real important to us. It gives us access to a lot of different things. I have a basket of corn, a basket of potatoes, and two chickens in the car right now. That's standard trade for delivering two babies." Doc changed the subject, "Where do you get fuel for the airplane?"

"From underground storage tanks."

"I thought that stuff was all used up?" Doc said.

"I think it be all gone except for what the government had squirreled away."

"Isn't it too old to burn?"

"It's stabilized," Pete answered, "and we can fix that."

"It must burn alright or ya' wouldn't be flying. I have a hard time getting the old flivver to burn the gas that I use. Some mornings she sure enough fights turning over.

I don't know whether it's getting to be like me or I'm getting to be like it.

"Matt and me could check out the motor for you."

"Who's Matt?" the old man asked.

"My wife's brother. He understands motors and mechanical things," Pete said, following a big gulp of coffee. "Where did you come by coffee this good?"

"Traded for it. Mostly it's food or fiber if it's local, but once in a while some brave soul will bring a boatload of trade goods up the coast from Mexico or beyond. They will have coffee beans and tea leaves in their trade goods. We give them alcohol, corn or wheat if they need it, and cattle. Meat on the hoof is a big item. And, they will give you anything for a horse. A virus passed around by mosquitoes keeps killing off their horses."

"Do you trade with these people?" Pete asked.

"No," Doc said, "but I treat people that do."

"Do you camp here a lot?"

"It's a regular stopping place when I'm making my rounds. Yesterday I was delivering babies on a ranch southwest of here. Delivering one is unusual enough. I delivered two yesterday, and they was both good, strong babies. Course, they was both out of migrant workers from up north.

"It makes me think that things have changed. Time was when people up north had fertility problems. Even the birds and fish had it. They had all kinds of trouble with miscarriage. Now, their babies are healthier than ours.

"They said ya' could watch the fish up there and tell how things were going to be in people. I don't know if ya' could do that or not but it sounded official-like. And, some salmon had big tumors on their heads . . . saw 'em myself. There's still places up there that people have to avoid."

"Jane tells the same kind of stories about her part of the country."

Doc finished his sandwich and washed it down with a big gulp of coffee.

"In the fire light, the flyin' machine looks new and so do your clothes."

"Not new, just unused," Pete said.

The old doctor leaned back against a rock and lit his pipe.

I suppose ya' heard about the Ghost City Mob?"

"The Ghost City Mob be dead and gone," Pete said.

"What happened?"

"Chinese killed 'em off last spring."

"How did they get involved with the Chinese?"

"I don't know the details. Jane will tell you about it tomorrow."

"I'm going to meet your people tomorrow?"

Pete wiped the sauce from his cheek.

"I'm thinking on it if you be goin' our way. Your car needs to be looked at, and Jane wants to learn healing."

"I suspect ya' want to trade one for the other, and I'm not sure I want to do that. I don't know who ya' folks are."

Pete didn't answer. He looked into the fire wondering if he said something wrong.

"My father drummed medicine into my head from my eighth birthday on. I know all there is to know about the human body, both male and female, in sickness and health. I make my own medicines, I run my own tests, and I do surgery on any part of the body. Your Jane, whoever she is, doesn't have enough time left to learn what I know about medicine.

"I'd wager that none of you young people have done anything that could compare with that kind of dedication."

Pete sat quietly for a minute. When he replied he spoke softly.

"Where I'm from an old man be respected for his wisdom. It be something that a person earns, and they be expected to help the young ones learn.

"You've proven yourself, but no matter how very wise and dedicated a healin' man you be, you would lose your wager.

"As good as you are at saving life, I be better takin' it away."

Pete was trying hard to keep the fire out of his words.

"My training began when I be two, my toys be real guns, and I killed the enemy by the time I be five. Now, my enemies be dead.

"When I met Jane I be little more than an animal. Now, she be my wife, and I know ways other than killing. If you ain't interested in teachin', your way be different from mine, but I'll be lookin' for another doctor that will. She be havin' her chance to learn!"

The old doctor couldn't hold back the smug look that took over his face, and he patted his knee while he puffed on his pipe.

"I knew ya'd tell me who ya' were if I riled ya' a little. The way ya' came out of that airplane door made me suspicious, and your eyes tell me that ya' came from the desert. I wondered if ya' wasn't clan. Don't take what I said to heart.

"I tried to help a desert warrior years ago. He took a bullet near the heart, and I would have saved him if he had stayed down and let himself heal. Your eyes remind me of his."

"What clan?" Pete asked.

"I'll tell ya' the whole story someday, it's a good story but it's kind of long," Doc said, smiling. "How did a wild spirit like yourself let a girl get her hooks into ya'?"

"I'll tell ya' the whole story someday, it be a good story but it be kind'a long," Pete said.

Doc puffed again on the old pipe.

"This brings to mind a phrase from the original oath that doctors take, it's a promise to pass on knowledge to the next generation. Ma and I don't have children, and I never had a student. If Jane has the interest I'll make time to teach her as much as I can."

"We be havin' a baby," Pete said. "Jane be havin' someone to teach."

"So much the better. Have ya' both got good genes?" Doc tapped his pipe on a rock.

Pete frowned.

"What?"

"Do ya' have diseases that are passed from parents to children."

Pete still didn't understand so Doc explained.

"For example, I know a disease where the lungs get plugged up, and another where sugar builds up in the blood. Some men can't get bleeding to stop and others got no immunity. Children suffer most, and they often die early.

"I've been watching a real common disease in boys. It seems that the growth of blood vessels to the heart muscle slows down growing by the time they reach five or six years of age. This prevents the heart from growing to its normal size. They literally outgrow their own heart. That's why we have more young women than young men."

"Matt's wife took care of a boy like that," Pete said.

"In a town up north some of the girls have a problem with fat," Doc said. "They start growing fat tumors when they're young if they ain't watched. They go kind of crazy for fat."

"Jane ain't said anything about her family, but I gotta a half-brother that's albino. I'll be fightin' him to the death one day."

Doc was fiddling with his pipe when Pete asked another question.

"What do you think caused my desert?"

"It has to do with the sun and changes in the sky," Doc said. "It's a complicated story."

"I tried to read about deserts but I didn't understand much of it from my word books. I liked the picture books better. Albedo helps me but he be too smart to understand."

"Who is Albedo?" Doc asked.

"Albedo be a computer that raised me after everyone left," Pete said.

"I know a woman that trades books," Doc said. "One day we'll see what she has on the subject. It's kind of funny, her first place got burned out and all her books turned to ash except for this one book and she traded it to me to have a tooth pulled. It ain't doing me any good so I think I'll give it to you and maybe your Albedo can make sense out of it."

The next morning Pete was away at first light. He was feeling pleased with himself because he had a good conversation with Doc Welty. He was a crafty old guy that could teach Jane a great deal.

Doc Welty eventually arrived at Pete's camp and met his family. Pete and Matt worked on Doc's old car while Jane and the doctor discussed the possibility of her learning medicine while helping with his medical practice.

After the good doctor left, Pete and Matt took some of the family on an airplane trip. Bobbie and Rona Ti decided to get a hot bath and a long, dry nap.

After unpacking and bathing, and after stretching out on their cots, Rona Ti brought up something that had been on her mind for many days.

"Bobbie, I have hard question . . . How I become breeder girl?"

Bobbie was surprised.

"Are you sure that you shouldn't wait. After all, you're young and a ruler in your country."

"Woman ruler not all same as man ruler," Rona Ti said. "Like breeze holding up kite, woman not seen, hold son up in mind of people, protect image. Woman watch till son old enough for leader, then council, support, protect back.

"If no son, Priests give me to some old boss mans. They old, soft, have many wives. Young mans have no wives. If I have baby son, promise be kept, son be God-King. I chose young mans for me.

"What I do first?"

"Well, first you need to let people know that you want to be a breeder girl, and you've done that by telling me. I'm sure that Matt will help you if it's him that you're interested in. After all, I was a breeder girl and his father had a breeder girl. Do you want me to ask him for you?"

"Matt very desirable," Rona Ti said, carefully. "Him strong, intelligent, most handsome. Matt light hair, blue eyes. Pete dark hair, dark eyes."

"If you would rather be a breeder girl for Pete I'll ask Jane when the time is right," Bobbie said. "If by chance there is a problem, we will find someone for you out here."

Winter weather wasn't far off, and Jane guessed that the family would not be traveling for a while. Doc made a place for Jane and her family in a vacant house in the small town of Sequoia Hill on the southwestern slope of the Sierra Nevada Range. The house was furnished and it came with a barn and a garage that provided protection that Matt and Pete needed to work on airplanes and cars.

Life had been good and the whole west coast adventure was all Jane could have asked for. She worked seven days a week with the doctor, the whole family got wet on a sandy Pacific Coast beach, and Pete hadn't found it necessary to kill anyone, yet.

Doc's little hospital was the biggest thing in town, but once a month traders came to town and Sequoia Hill became a market place. Pete didn't like crowds, but he was interested in men's competition events that were held in the afternoon and evening of trade day.

These people can make a contest out of anything, Pete thought. *They make fun out of challenging one another and no one takes the fighting seriously.* Pete watched but he was careful about the contests that he entered. Running and wrestling were two events that he allowed himself to enter. Matt had to watch over Pete to be sure he was able to turn off the aggression when his matches were over. No surprise.

Bobbie stayed home most of the time. Trade day wasn't fun for her. She was getting so big and eyes followed her because pregnant woman were uncommon. Jane would soon understand because she was about two months behind Bobbie.

It was getting more and more difficult for Jane to be with Pete. She didn't want a time-out, but she realized that she needed one. This was the time that Jane had been waiting for, so with little ceremony she gave her blessing sending Pete and Rona Ti on a trip. It might have been more difficult if Rona Ti wasn't so much like a little sister.

Eventually Bobbie had a boy baby named Paul. Matt was pleased that the lad was strong and healthy. Two months later Jane gave birth to a beautiful, bald-headed daughter. Pete tried to hide his pride, but during his unguarded moments it slipped past the thin stoic shield that protected his emotions. Jane was relieved that he had not demanded a son.

Jane's baby girl was named Christy, and she had her father's eyes. Pete noticed but kept his thoughts to himself. It was good to have something that was shared by just the two of them. Pete speculated on the possibility of Rona

Ti's baby having the same kind of eyes. *No,* he thought, *her baby will look like her.*

Winter was mild and rainy and Matt needed something to fill his time. The family had seen all that they came west to see, and the women were busy with babies and special interests. Pete had developed a dry, raspy cough and he decided to keep out of the weather for a while. Matt decided to look around for someone to talk about west-coast trade possibilities.

It was on Matt's first solo trip that he ran into trouble.

Chapter 21

Low hanging clouds had kept Matt near the ground and regrettably he had been unable to keep track of landmarks. Matt promptly went to his map when he realized he was lost.

When Matt glanced up from his map, he saw that his airplane was closing in on rooftops of a small town. Without warning the motor sputtered quickly forcing him to scan the area for a place to land.

When the hum of the motor returned Matt gained altitude and the incident was shrugged off. The next time the motor sputtered it died and Matt was unable to restart it.

A quick check of the gauges told Matt that the oil pressure was up, the battery was charged, and he had plenty of fuel. Radio contact had been lost two days earlier so he would have to land in a strange neighborhood.

The altitude Matt had gained gave him a good view of the countryside but he was having a problem keeping it out of the clouds.

Matt saw mountains on his right and ahead of him

was a valley with a stream flowing down the middle. He had been more or less following a road when he lost the motor, but he couldn't judge how level it was. Still the road would be smoother than a pasture.

Matt came in low and fast. He saw a road full of furrow and debris, but as far as he could tell he had no fault lines to dodge. Matt circled, dropped his flaps and came straight in. It was a rough ride but he was doing fine until the last few feet. The right wheel dropped in a rut and the rut led the airplane wheel into a chuckhole that was too deep to bounce over. The little airplane spun around and tipped forward on its nose.

The tire on the right wheel had blown and the landing gear was bent, but Matt was most uneasy about the propeller. It was stuck in the mud and it might be bent.

Matt had been walking for two days, and he verified an observation that he had made from the airplane. He was alone.

It wasn't the coldest part of the winter, but it was a little more than cool. His clothing was not made for a winter walk, but as long as he kept moving he didn't suffer. In the evenings he found shelter in deserted buildings, and he used wood from a building to make a fire.

It was near noon of the third day when Matt came upon an old man watching a flock of sheep. The white haired old man was concentrating on his pipe although he knew Matt was coming. The old man chose to ignore him.

"Hello," Matt said. He spoke louder than normal as one is apt to do with older people. "Nice looking Suffolk sheep. Where's your dog?"

The old man looked off toward the mountains.

"Don't have to yell at me. I hear just fine, and I ain't got need of no dog. What's a person like yourself doin' wonderin' 'round my place?"

"My airplane went down, and I'm looking for transportation back to Sequoia Hill."

"You a long way from home to be hoofin' it," the old man said. "What you need is a horse."

"What I need is a new landing gear and maybe a propeller," Matt said.

It was a minute or two before the old man spoke.

"What is it that takes ya' way from Sequoia Hill?"

"I've been looking for someone that trades down south," Matt said. "Mister, I surely could use something to eat."

"Your hands and pockets look mighty empty for a person that's wantin' so many things," the old man said.

"I know things and that don't leave a bump in your pocket," Matt said, making the old man smile. "I know you smoke a pipe, that means you're a tradin' man. I know you're a sheep man that ain't got sheepdogs, and I know where there will be two litters of sheepdogs come spring. A male from one litter and a female from the other litter would make a sheepdog breeder out of a man."

"Knowin' is good, but I don't hear any barkin'. Do you know Doc Welty?" the sheepherder asked.

"He's teaching medicine to my sister," Matt answered, "and he kind of takes care of the rest of us. I keep his old car running."

"I guess if you're a friend of Doc's I can feed you and help you with a ride," the old man said. "Won't find any airplane parts though. Is it true about the puppies, they're natural sheep dogs and you're goin' to bring me two of them?"

"It's true," Matt declared. "I saw their parents work sheep myself. I'll fly the pups over to you as soon as they're weaned. We have a second airplane in case mine ain't fixed."

The old sheepherder thought a while.

"Are you sure that a ride and a meal is enough for two sheepdogs. I don't want my dogs to sound cheap when I brag about the trade."

"I'd take a horse?"

"A horse for two dogs. Ain't that a little lopsided?"

"You just said that you didn't want the dogs to sound cheap."

Matt was trying to sweeten the deal.

"To top it off, I'll give back the horse after I'm done with him."

The old sheepherder summed it up.

"So, in short, you want somethin' to eat and a horse to ride back to Doc's place?"

"For two sheepdog puppies."

"What if I said I'd take ya there myself, along with a load of my animals to go at the next trade day?"

"I'd say done."

"And, done it is," the old man echoed.

After they shook hands on the deal the white haired old man ushered Matt up to his cabin in the pine trees. A young woman came to the door as Matt and the old man led the sheep into a fenced watering pen.

Matt followed the old man up to the porch. The young woman wasn't happy.

"Why are you bringing a white man up to our house?"

"Bee, we don't turn away a hungry man when we have food left over at every meal," the old man said, frowning at the young woman.

"You want to feed a white man knowin' how they treated us? Skeeter, you're nothin' but an old fool!"

"I beg your pardon Miss Bee," Skeeter said, fixing to correct the young woman. "This man ain't treated nobody no way 'round here. He's a trader friend of Doc Welty. We got a deal goin' and bein' fed is part of the deal. He ain't had no vittles for two-and-a-half days.

"You can't go around hatin' all whites because of a few bad ones. What if this man hated us folks 'cause a black man robbed him in the past? We couldn't 'a made this deal that's goin' to get us two sheepdog puppies. Not only that, me and him is goin' to get a load of sheep to trade day at Sequoia Hill."

"How you goin' to get a load of sheep past Faulty's Greens country?" Bee asked.

"He's from Sequoia Hill and he needs a ride home. He'll get us through alright. He was in that airplane we saw a few days ago. He broke his flying machine and he can't fly out of here until he gets it fixed. I don't even know his name."

Matt was quick to introduce himself.

"I'm Matt Blacktower from back east. I spent thirty some years on the trek working in the field and trading with farmers."

The young woman was less hostile.

"I'm sorry if I rub ya the wrong way, bein' light-haired

163

and blue-eyed and with your new clothes and all. You ain't carryin' much for a trader."

"I had to land on the road about two-and-a-half days north of here," Matt explained. "I wasn't looking to trade on this trip. I wanted to find a trader."

The old man butted in.

"I got some business to tend in the community, so Bee, here, will see to it that you get somethin' to eat and drink. Bee, fix him up a pallet by the fireplace. It's too cold to sleep outside. Matt, the people I trade with call me Skeeter, and if I'm lucky we'll be on the road first thing in the mornin'. Bee, call your kids in from the trees and have the boys chop some firewood. The girl can take the sheep out on the grass. There's still some green patches if they go far enough out."

Bee was busy cooking up a big pot of mutton stew and tortillas while Matt watched anxiously. She placed a big glass of lemonade on the table in front of him.

"If you ain't had food in several days you probably ain't had much to drink either."

Two boys and a girl watched as Matt tried to sip the drink, and they laughed as he lost control and downed the entire drink on the second sip.

Matt got to his feet and looked at the young man in the doorway.

"Let's go chop some firewood, I can't stand being where there's cooking going on."

Bee's attitude had changed; she was almost pleasant.

"Here's some corn bread and butter to eat on the way. I'll call when the stew's ready. And, about Faulty's Greens, we'll talk about them this evening."

Matt sharpened axes while he stuffed his mouth.

When the axes were sharp enough he looked at the young man and nodded his head. It was warm and sunny in the wood lot and Matt took off his shirt. His muscles bulged as he swung the ax and the young man watched. In two hours they had enough wood to last Bee a week in her cook stove.

"How do you get muscles like that?" the boy asked.

"Putting up hay, digging drainage ditches, scooping grain, digging postholes, chopping wood, building barns, and fighting."

"I thought you was a trader?" the boy asked.

"I am a trader," Matt explained. "Trading was like dancing, we saved both for the end of day. We worked hard on whatever had to be done while we had light."

"That sounds like my dad. He had muscles like yours."

"I thought Skeeter was your pa."

"Skeeter is my gramps. Greens was ready to runoff with my ma and my sister and pa stopped them. Faulty's Greens killed my pa a couple of years back."

"Who are these people?" Matt said, shaking his head.

"They camp way south of here. Some thinks they're a militia of some kind, but they got no bullets. They're white with blue eyes. They got hair on their faces but none on their heads. They steal women and sell um in town. The Canadians don't put up with them at all. They shoot at them for just hanging around."

"No wonder I made your mother nervous," Matt said.

The next morning Matt had to dip his head in the stock tank to wake himself. After his stomach was full of bacon and grits he was ready to go. Skeeter had a big wagon loaded with sheep and it was pulled by two horses.

"I got the use of an extra horse by takin' three old ewes and two young rams for another sheep herder," Skeeter explained. "And I may have a line on airplane parts. A man over in Spanish Town said he knowed about a airplane scrap yard down in the desert beyond the western mountains. The only problem being that it's on the west side of the fault. He told me how to get there in case you was interested."

"Your grandson told me about Faulty's Greens," Matt said. "It was bad what they did to your family. Did you take it to the law?"

"Ain't no law here abouts," Skeeter said. "Didn't need law until that bunch moved in. Some people from our community caught a couple of theirs on the road alone, and they was made to pay for the killin' spree they went on. Now, they just sneak around tryin' to grab a woman now-and-again."

Matt was talking to himself.

"Sounds like trouble makers."

Matt and Skeeter had been on the road nearly two days when they came to a good hardtop road. Skeeter said that it would take a little longer but it would be a smoother ride. In the evening the animals were allowed to graze while the men made camp by a stream.

Near midnight Matt hobbled the animals and put another log on the fire. He stretched out on his blanket and turned his back to the fire.

The morning sun had warmed Matt but it was an unusually loud sound that brought him to his feet. He tried to jump up but his feet were bound together and he fell forward giving the appearance of being clumsy.

Matt looked up at Skeeter and got no signal about what was going on. Then he heard two of the intruders laughing behind him. Matt looked over his shoulder and frowned at what he saw. Eight or ten oddly dressed men were loading Skeeter's wagon. One of them held the other end of the rope that was around Matt's ankles.

Matt took off the rope and got to his feet. He carefully coiled the rope as he walked forward. The intruder thought he had pulled a trick on one of his own. He laughed and pounded his leg.

As Matt handed him the rope he swung a fist from the other side flattening the prankster.

Fighting among these folks must be as common as eating and drinking. They must be Faulty's Greens, Matt thought, *and they think I'm one of them. They're big, and they look strong. Two or three I could handle but not ten. There'll be even more of them back in their camp. They're going to do something to Skeeter."*

Matt gathered up the rope and tied one end around Skeeter's neck, and he pulled him to his feet.

Matt's wink told Skeeter to go along.

"Why are you letting them do all the work. Load the sheep, hook up the horses and get my food ready."

Skeeter acted very humble, and he did as he was told.

A tall and husky man approached Matt.

"What're you doing out here alone?"

Matt sized up the fellow. His manner and tone of voice told Matt that he was probably the leader, and fighting him might keep the rest of them out of the fight until it was over.

"I'm taking sheep to trade day at Sequoia Hill."

"When did you let your hair grow out?" the intruder asked.

"When I took a wife I went to trading. I did better when I didn't look like you."

"I suppose people like them are tellin' you what to do."

"Where I'm from no body tells folks what to do."

Matt decided to question his leadership.

"How often do you people eat? Are you eating cabbage or steak? What do you drink, whisky or musty old home brew beer? I don't see any ammo in your belts. When was the last time you were with a nice woman? Why don't you have good things? Now, think about who's bossin' you around. Is he lazy and soft in the head? Do you need a new leader?"

"And, you think that your it?" the big guy asked.

"I've got ammunition for my guns, and I eat good three times a day. I've got a pretty woman and a healthy son, and I got a place called home.

"Let me see if I can describe your action. You live off of what you can steal and that ain't been much lately what with the Canadians shooting at you. You don't hunt or farm because it's too much work. You sit around and drink and fight, and then you sit around some more.

"Your clothes are dirty, you haven't eaten off a clean dish in years, and I can't even guess what kind of a woman would want you. You're all old men and there ain't any young ones coming up. It won't be long until you don't even exist anymore, and I bet that none of this ever crossed your mind."

Matt was ready to climb aboard the wagon when the big Skinhead spun him around.

"Get off the wagon this is our stuff."

Matt came around swinging, but the big guy was ready for him and blocked his arm. He caught Matt on the forehead with his own punch. The attacker followed with a kick to the legs intended to put Matt on the ground. Matt braced himself, caught the man's belt and flung him over his shoulder. The big guy landed with a crash on his own back.

Matt backed off. He wanted the fight to last. It had been over a year since his last brawl and this was going to be a good one.

Matt caught movement out of the corner of his eye. He ducked forward feeling the breeze of a tree branch whiz by his head.

The big guy has a friend, Matt thought.

When the branch didn't work, the second attacker pulled a knife and stepped forward swinging his weapon. Matt dodged the swing, caught the man's wrist, and spun him around. He twisted the hand pointing the blade at the man's chest and pulled as hard as he could on the arm. The blade lodged between two ribs and the helper dropped out of the fight.

Matt looked at the others and spoke through clinched teeth.

"The rest of you keep out!"

The big man had struggled to his feet, and this time he was a little less sure of himself. The two men circled each other, flicking out a hand now and then while they looked for a weakness.

Matt ducked inside of a headshot and hit his opponent three times at the lower edge of the rib cage. The man winced on the third blow. Matt hit him once more in the same place just for punishment.

As Matt spun away he took a punishing blow in the middle of the back. He dropped to his knees. Before Matt could recover he was captured under the big guy's arm, and he was driven back into the wagon wheel. It was Matt's turn to gasp for air.

Matt held on tightly to the wagon wheel and looked up to see a hard baldhead about to hammer him in the face. Matt turned in time to keep his nose from being flattened. Mister baldhead missed his target and plowed, head first, into a brace holding a water barrel.

While the man's hand was up rubbing the top of his head Matt jumped to his feet. He put everything he had into one last punch in the stomach. The attacker stood there doubled over hugging his gut.

Matt wiped blood from the corner of his mouth ready to continue the fight. Faulty's man dropped to his knees, held up his hand, and signaled that the fight was over.

Matt climbed up to the wagon's driver's bench and spoke loud enough for all to hear.

"Who's next?"

No one stepped forward to take up the fight.

"If this is over I want you to split up and get out of here. There's women out there, find one for yourself."

Skeeter was going over events in his mind as they continued on their trip. He wanted to have things in their proper order when he got home. He had enough story material for two Sunday afternoons and the trip was barely started.

"Matt, you a lucky man," Skeeter said. "If that bull of a man had butted you instead of the water barrel, you'd be takin' angel lessons about now."

Skeeter chuckled.

"Neither one of you got punched in the jaw. I'd give a wagonload of sheep to see that last punch of yours land on his jaw instead of his stomach. I promise, I never saw a person hit that hard. It sounded like someone hit a hollow tree with a sledgehammer. I decided to remember that sound."

Skeeter talked about the fight and Faulty's Greens the rest of the day, and it dawned on him that Matt put a rope around his neck.

"Matt, why did you put a rope around my neck?"

Matt thought a minute.

"A friend of mine taught me that. It was a symbol in his part of the country. If your rope was on someone you were responsible for that person as long as you was alive."

Late afternoon had Skeeter guiding his team of horses up a side road.

"We be makin' camp in a couple hours. It'll be dark by the time we get there. I'll point out some things to you in the mornin'. Probably won't be able to see nothin' tonight."

"I hope I don't wake to a surprise like this morning."

Skeeter emphasized his thoughts.

"Oh, I guarantee you won't wake up to a surprise like what you had this mornin'."

Chapter 22

The sun was up before Matt opened his eyes. He heard some shuffling of feet by the fire and he heard Skeeter chuckling to himself. He should get up, splash cold water on his face, and help Skeeter get ready to go. Just then, someone lifted the edge of his blanket and looked at Matt. Skeeter busted out laughing as Matt pushed himself back.

Two, puffy, little eyes watched Matt's eyes widen as he gradually realized they were not alone. The childish face looked swollen, and a pair of eyes closed when the face smiled. The little girl and her companions stepped back when Matt sat up and looked around.

Early morning air was heavy with fog. It just hung there like a pair of wet drawers. Matt shivered and he heard morning greetings from the children. He nodded his head in return.

The night before several young ladies had fallen asleep watching Skeeter's campfire from their bedroom window, and this morning, some of them didn't bother to change into day clothes before they came down to greet their visitors. The girls had on hooded capes against the cold mist, and some wore play pants while others obviously did not. Two of the younger girls wore oversized nightgowns with hems dragging in wet grass and dirt.

Skeeter was watching over the top plank in the wagon box, and he was laughing at Matt's surprise. Matt hollered over his shoulder.

"Skeeter, who are these people?"

Skeeter had been slicing bacon into a skillet, and now it was ready to go on the fire.

"We camped right on the edge of a little town, and I thought you might like to meet some of the residents. They've lived here as long as anyone can remember.

"It seems like half of the town's daughters don't turn out right and proper once they start to become young women. It has somethin' to do with fat. Watch when they get a whiff of what's cookin' on the fire. I'll have to take it off the fire or they could burn theirselves. They don't let 'em eat fat over at their treatment center because it puffs 'em up like they was snakebit. They get to cravin' fat somethin' fierce."

Matt looked a little bewildered.

"Why are you making bacon for them if they aren't supposed to eat fat?"

"It's the only way to get 'em out from under those capes so we can see what they look like," Skeeter said. "It don't last long, the keepers will be out to find 'em any minute now."

The smell was creating a great hunger in the young girls. They pushed off their hoods and looked left and right trying to find the source. It was then that Matt got his first good look at the girls.

"They call those big round bumps 'fat tumors.' My wife had a small one on her hip so I know what they look like.

"The older ones that's still livin' know better than to get after fat the way them younger ones does. Once they get to be grown they spend their days in a rockin' chair on the porch, and once rockin' sets in they usually don't live very long."

"You've done this before haven't you?" Matt asked.

"I've been down here a time or two on my way to trade day," Skeeter said. "That bacon's gettin' mighty temptin'. You gonna be in the way any minute now."

Skeeter cut the bacon into smaller sections and scattered them on a big rock behind Matt and the girls pushed and shoved to get at the greasy little chunks of meat.

The two men were ignored as long as the bacon lasted. Skeeter had to hide the frying pan because he knew there would eventually be a fight over it.

When the breakfast bell sounded at their home, the girls tried to find clean spots on their capes to wipe off their faces and hands. They pulled up their hoods and tried to adjust their clothing as if to hide what they had been doing.

A few minutes after the girls had departed a stern-faced, older woman found her way to Skeeter's wagon. The frying pan was back on the fire and Matt was watching their breakfast cook while Skeeter gathered his livestock.

"Did you give bacon to my girls?" the stern said asked.

"I didn't," Matt said.

"Don't try to hide Skeeter. I know it was you behind

this." The woman looked at Matt. "He knows the girls can't have greasy food. It makes their tumors grow. They spend most of their lives giving up fat. Then, along comes Skeeter and sets us back a whole year."

"I'm not sure I understand the problem," Matt said.

Please come to the home," the woman said. "Meet the people that have to deal with this particular problem everyday of their lives. Two of the older girls that live at the clinic are my daughters. Skeeter, I would like for you to meet them, they remember you."

Old Skeeter looked down.

"We'll stop in for a minute before we leave. We got to get to Sequoia Hill for trade day, and they ain't much time for pleasantries. I'll leave you an old mutton ewe for all the trouble I caused."

After the wagon was loaded and ready to go Skeeter pulled into the driveway and sat in the wagon. The stern lady came to the front door and invited the travelers to get down from the wagon.

"Come meet my two older girls."

The mother's pride in the young women was obvious.

"You can see that, by withholding fatty food, it is possible for the girls to look quite nice. You would never guess how old they are because they don't show their age much beyond mid-teens. They're both in their thirties." The lady looked down and her voice quivered a little. "They don't have much time left."

As nice as the daughters looked, Matt saw something strange in their eyes. It wasn't five minutes later that this strangeness expressed itself. Both girls slipped up on the backside of Skeeter and started tearing at his old denim coat. In a matter of seconds the attack turned vicious, with guttural whoops and growls as they took old Skeeter to the ground. Then, they turned on each other.

Matt pulled Skeeter to his feet and lifted him up to the wagon seat.

"What was that all about?"

Skeeter had to take a minute to catch his breath.

"Don't ask me. Those people never attacked anyone before that I know of. Those two little girls was strong, now. They put me on my back! Not many grown men can do that."

"Why were they after your coat?" Matt asked.

"I can't figure it out," Skeeter responded. "They almost tore the pockets clear off."

"What did you have in your pockets?"

"I had a little wedge of fried mush and a couple of chunks of bacon left over from breakfast, but they was wrapped up in a cloth. I was savin' 'em for a little midmornin' pick-me-up. That's no reason to be jumped on."

"I think it's time for us to be on our way," Matt said.

Skeeter was feeling bad about what happened.

"Let me leave one of these old ewes for causin' trouble."

"Why don't you put three of them out?" Matt said. "I'll pay you for the other two."

Two days later Skeeter and Matt rode down the street in Sequoia Hill. Skeeter spoke quietly to Matt.

"Matt, did you notice the man across the street on the corner? It almost looked like he nodded at us. Did he nod at us?"

Matt smiled.

"Yes, he's my sister's husband."

"His eyes don't miss much do they?" Skeeter said. "He looks mean enough to spit nails."

"It isn't so much that he's mean," Matt said. "He's just very serious. He's from the Red Clay Desert."

"I heard stories about that place," Skeeter said, "don't want to go there."

Skeeter was hesitant as he and Matt approached Pete.

"Pete, I want you to meet the man that took me in and brought me back here. This is Skeeter. He herds sheep on the far side of the valley."

Pete about crushed Skeeter's hand.

"If you be Matt's friend you be my friend. We thank you for your hospitality. You come trade stories with us tonight over dinner."

Skeeter started to say something, but he changed his mind and cleared his throat instead.

"Do you want to know what I see Mr. Skeeter?"

Skeeter wanted to look away, but he couldn't.

"Not if it ain't good," Skeeter spluttered. "I just wanted to do some tradin'."

"We can talk tradin' tonight," Pete said, looking back across town. "Do you see those two men dressed in black sitting on the bench under the big pine tree? They belong to a group out of the Bitterroot Mountains and they be askin' for women. Does that sound familiar, Matt?"

"It sounds like something Ard knows about if he was a mind to talk," Matt replied.

"I don't like those two," Pete said. "What do you think about folks like that, Mister Skeeter?"

"Are they carryin' guns?" Skeeter asked.

"Yes," Pete said. "They got guns."

"Well, they ain't afraid of nobody sittin' out under a tree like that," Skeeter said. "I'd say dangerous pretty well sums it up."

Matt and Skeeter walked back to the wagon.

"Pete very seldom tells people his thoughts," Matt said. "He respects a man that's been around a long time. If you want to trade with us you have to understand Pete."

Skeeter smiled.

"It's easy to understand respect. I wish Bee could see this. Could be she'd learn that Skeeter ain't just an old house plant."

At dinner Matt declared that he dumped his airplane but Matt had a tendency to skim over things. When it was Skeeter's turn to talk it was easy to see that Skeeter understood the importance of a good story well told. It was news and entertainment. It was to be taken slowly and savored. The facts would be presented one at a time and they had to be almost true.

It had been a good trade day in Sequoia Hill. The sheep were sold and Matt was ready to find the airplane scrap yard, and Skeeter was going to point the way, but plans change.

Chapter 23

The men in black were right in the middle of the trade crowd when the older of the two strangers rose to his feet, unbuttoned his coat, and leisurely pulled out his revolver. He fired twice into the air to get everyone's attention.

"My people need women, old or young, fat or skinny, their looks ain't important. I know for a fact that you got four or five women for every man. I'm askin' nice for some of you women folks to come with us if you're wantin' a man for yourself. We pay top dollar to family heads if you got too many daughters livin' in your house."

People listened without comment as they passed, but none bothered to stop. The speaker looked around in disgust and climbed onto his horse.

"Remember," the man said. "We tried to do this the civilized way. When I return I won't be alone. If you hide we'll burn you out. If you run we'll chase you down. If we don't find enough women you will indulge one man and all of his brothers."

Pete's mind was on other things and he had nearly

forgotten about the men dressed in black. Pete heard the shots, but that wasn't unusual for trade day. When Skeeter came by looking for Matt, Pete stepped out on the front porch holding his baby daughter.

"What be the commotion down on the street," Pete said, looking toward the trade area.

"I think those men you was a watchin' tried to convert people to their way of thinkin'," Skeeter said, "but, no body was payin' attention and I think it bothered the head preacher man. He took to shootin' his revolver in the air.

"You goin' along with Matt and me to look for airplane parts?"

"I be staying behind. I don't trust someone shooting guns in a crowd. I might need a talk with those two."

From above the scrap yard looked huge. Matt circled the area several times, but he saw no people inside or outside of the boundary fence. The place appeared to be abandoned as were most of the properties on the west side of the big fault. The ground shook some, but for Matt, it was a matter of putting it out of his mind while he looked for his airplane parts.

Matt and Skeeter spent the better part of two days looking and collecting. Skeeter managed to salvage objects of interest from office buildings and houses. Bee and her kids would take their pick and the rest he saved for trade.

When Matt and Skeeter returned to Sequoia Hill they saw Pete sitting in his jeep north of town watching the main road. By the time Pete joined them at their landing field Matt was busy refueling the airplane and Skeeter was transferring duffel bags to his wagon.

"Did you find the parts you needed?" Pete asked.

"I think so," Matt said. "Actually, we found a whole lot of spare parts that we dropped off at Edwards. Found a welder that works." Matt looked at the jeep, "Why did you put the machine gun back on the jeep?"

"The men we be watchin' came back making serious threats about the women."

"I thought they left town."

"They did and I followed them north until I got rained out two days ago."

"What about the other town north of us?" Matt asked.

"They got the same threat."

"Have we got time to fix the airplane that I wrecked, or do you want to go after 'em right now?"

"We need to get both airplanes in the air."

All three men were needed to move the little airplane out of the pothole and replace the broken parts. As far as Matt could tell the motor and propeller were not damaged. The motor turned over and ran smoothly. Matt looked and listened but he could hear no unusual motor sounds. Still old fluid hoses and belts were replaced to be sure.

Matt was about to land at Sequoia Hill when Skeeter asked about an observation he had made.

"Does Pete cough like that a lot?"

"He's had a dry little cough that comes and goes. Why?"

"Listen to him on the radio," Skeeter said. "It's hard

for some folks to put up with cold, wet winters here. What does Doc have to say about it?"

"I don't think Doc Welty has looked at him," Matt said. "Don't sound that bad to me. Maybe he's got an allergy."

"I wouldn't think much of it," Skeeter said, "but I heard of folks that cough theirselves sick. Starts off small like this and gets worse until it gets in the way with breathin'.'"

"I'll get Doc to take a listen."

Pete and Skeeter had been flying together for two days before Pete spotted horse back riders nearly two hundred miles north of Sequoia Hill. The riders had just split up at a fork in the trail. Half of the column broke off to the east and the rest continued south.

"Looks like half of those riders is goin' to Sequoia Hill," Skeeter said.

"Matt and Bobbie will watch 'em from the other airplane. You and me need to warn the people over east! We'll help if they want help!"

Pete studied the people that had been told to bring their guns and gather at the airplane. They were poorly equipped to resist armed riders.

"You folks ain't got enough guns to stand up face to face with the likes of what be comin' at you and you can't let them into your town. They be wantin' women and they will be trying to take yours. Your best bet might be to hit and run out on the trail. If you do it right you can force them to camp out in the open come night fall, and if they do we'll get them."

As Pete turned to leave he added, "Make them fight on your terms, and pick your spots."

The afternoon ambush was a complete surprise to all the Crusaders of Job. That evening, by his campfire, the events of the ambush were played over and over in the mind of an old elder dressed in black. He was the only Crusaders of Job elder that had survived. His troop had never been challenged by men that ran after firing their first round of shots. Brotherhood companions, that had been riding at the head of the column, were the first to be shot out of the saddle. Now the old man was alone.

He was a hard-bitten old fox that knew better than to provide the town people with an easy target. He recognized a major mistake made by the crusaders. They had misjudged the town's men while the town's men had not misjudged them.

I will deliberate about what happened to us, the old man thought, *In the morning I will send out scouts and they will find the town's men. After we have taken vengeance for our loss we will send their women north, and we will burn the town to the ground.*

If they expect to take us while we sleep, they will find that we are ready for their treachery!

Sleep would not come easily to the gray old head. It was past midnight and a light breeze blew puffy little clouds across the face of a full moon. In the camp of Job's Crusaders lively shadows flickered and jumped about, and whispered voices could be heard from uncomfortable men trying to sleep in dark shadows. Guards posted at either end of camp were dozing by their fires, and one small campfire burned near the elder. Eventually the sounds of sleeping men filled the night.

All was quiet now. The last of the campfires would flare up now and again as a fresh breeze hit the embers. The old veteran slipped down into a semi-comfortable position with his head resting on a log. He pulled a blanket over his shoulders, and he joined his men in noisy slumber.

It wasn't long until the elder was squirming in his sleep. A sharp rock poked him in the back and he swore an oath. He asked himself why he had not noticed the rock when he rolled out his blankets. Minutes later a stick caught in his blanket and it irritated him when he moved. Next his nose was being tickled. He puffed air from his mouth to blow it away. Something was crawling on his face. No. Someone was whispering in his ear.

"If you want to live, take your men out of this country and don't be comin' back."

The elder swung his left elbow back into Pete's face. As the old man rolled through the embers of the fire he came to his knees and drew his revolver.

"Go back to your hell, Satan!" the old fighter yelled. "Attack! Attack! The enemy is among us!"

A heavy knife came twirling over the flickering embers and the blade cut deeply into the elder's hand. The old man's first shot was straight up in the air. Pete was gone by the time the elder changed hands and cocked the gun for a second shot. Almost instantly, the camp came alive with random activity. Men, yelling and shooting, charged around looking for someone to fight but they had no targets.

Pete called from behind a tree.

"Old man, take your people and go or you'll die! You be the Satan not me."

The elder stood and emptied his revolver in the

direction of the voice. Pete ducked and two of the raiders fell wounded by wild shots from their leader.

"You were warned," Pete said, to himself as he lifted the quiet one and stepped out into the moonlight.

The elder didn't know what hit him, but he heard a popping sound and he felt the heat of the fire on his face.

Pete charged through the shadows of the surrounding scrub forest at the edge of camp. Men hiding in the trees neither saw nor heard Pete until he was beside them. Then it was too late.

On the far end of camp, Pete jumped a log and tumbled into a streambed where crusaders had picketed horses. Pete's first clip was empty and he reached for his knife as a wild-eyed raider stormed blindly into the shadows behind him.

Pete's knife wasn't there, and the raider was shooting his direction.

Bullets kicked gravel into Pete's face as he squirmed back into the weeds. Before the man could lever another shell into the chamber, he was hit from behind with a big stick.

Pete popped in another clip, and he was on his way before the guard hit the ground. As he crossed to the tree line on the other side of camp Pete could hear Skeeter yelling.

"I don't hold with hittin' folks from behind, but you earned it. What kind a people is takin' women from their homes the way you do? Now, you goin' to be stopped, 'cause you ain't got no idea about me and Pete, do ya? We just practice on the likes of you."

Several of the younger men had dropped their guns

and ran for the horses, and Skeeter had them all gathered in the streambed. When it was over, fewer than half of the original group was left to bury the dead and care for the wounded. After words were spoken over the dead the brotherhood was pointed toward home and urged not to delay for the sake of their wounded.

Pete held a cloth on his eye as he watched the column go out of sight.

"What happened to your eye?" Skeeter asked, "You have blood spots all over your face."

"The guard you thumped kicked up rocks into my face. Only one is causing any problem. It got me in the upper eyelid."

"Let me look at it." Skeeter said, wiping away the blood, "It almost went clear through your eyelid, but it's outside the eyeball. It'll heal."

"Can you get it out?" Pete asked.

"Probably fall off on its own if you let it alone."

Pete relaxed for a while after the men in black were gone. This gave his eye time to heal, but his cough continued.

Rona Ti gave birth to her son and Pete named him Haze Ti.

As winter months passed restlessness caused an obvious irritation in Pete's family. Matt's behavior become that of a caged lion and Pete had to leave the house daily for a long run. The girls were prone to argue and the children were fussy.

Pete realized that the time had come to leave Sequoia Hill. Pete had his people ready to go when Doc approached.

"Pete, before you git on your way," Doc said, "I got

something for you to give to Albedo. This is the book that I told you about. See if he can figure it out."

On the first day of the trip Pete and Matt flew the two older children and Jane's medical supplies to Ard's ranch. The men planned to return to the overpass bridges and spend time with the Planter's while they waited for Jane to pull up in the jeep. Pete's family was there but the Planters were gone.

The next morning about sunrise, Pete thought he could see something moving far out in the desert south of their camp. Jane heard their names before she could see who was calling. She soon recognized the Planter's children running to meet them. The children greeted their friends as expected, however Jane detected unhappiness in the children, and more than one asked Matt and Bobbie not to go.

The trip would have to wait.

A few minutes behind the children, Grandfather Young's family found Rona Ti and the old fellow got right to the point.

"We have lived for many, many years as you see us now. We welcome everyone in our camp and we respect everyone. We have never tried to persuade others to take up our beliefs although we tell them if they ask. It is best to be superior in your own way than to be inferior in the way of others. We have always listened with great interest to stories told by others because we learn from them. Also, we enjoy telling our stories when they finish. This is the way it has been for as long as I can remember."

The old man was searching for a way to introduce the problem.

"A man came to us out of the desert. He wore a tattered, black robe and a serape of rabbit skins. He was made welcome and he shared our food and our fire. He listened to our stories, and we listened to his stories.

"It wasn't long until he was the only one telling stories, and it became obvious that he was not satisfied with who we were. His stories changed to prayers, and they were long, painful prayers that frightened people. Some families left on the south road because of this strange man.

"For nearly a year, he has preached about the end of the world. He wants us to make sacrifices to make ourselves acceptable for the second coming, which is anytime now. We don't know what to do. He quotes the bible and there are those that think he is right."

"Does the man have a large hooked nose?" Rona Ti asked.

"Yes," the old man replied. "He spoke of the devil and he ran when he saw your airplane."

"The man is Father Seer," Rona Ti said. "He and his men kidnapped three of us and they tried to sacrifice us to a volcano. I have a scar as a reminder."

That night by the camp fire Matt and Pete volunteered to find Padre Seer. Matt knew that Pete would not be satisfied with just following the Planters. *Jane will have to keep Pete out of it*, Matt thought.

Pete tried to hide his cough, but Jane wasn't fooled. She feared pneumonia and she knew it to be a sure killer if she didn't fight it. Jane knew that Pete thought a lot about what the preacher did and he would push himself until he finished what he had started.

Jane made it very simple.

"Fight after you heal or your own lungs will kill you! Let Matt bring in the preacher."

Jane, Rona Ti and the babies left with Pete in one of the airplanes. Matt and Bobbie used the other airplane and the jeep to hunt the desert for signs of the priest, but they were too high or too fast to see details.

Matt parked under a railroad bridge well ahead of the Planter's caravan and Bobbie returned to a wagon driven by Grandfather Young. Matt had decided to keep out of sight in the desert well behind the last wagon.

I'll go back to the place where Father Seer ran off into the desert, Matt thought. *It isn't that far back and it's just possible that he's going the other direction.*

Planter wagons were two days away from the airplane and jeep, and Matt was about ready to concede that the Priest had gone west. Then he stepped on a boot track paralleling the road. Matt decided to follow tracks back to the camp instead of getting into a desert chase the other direction.

It took a day of backtracking to find out that the last wagon was helping him, and he was returning to the same wagon almost every night.

If he comes into camp late enough no one will see him, Matt thought, *they never post a night guard. Seer is on his way again before anyone is up. The people in the last wagon are helping him. Are they the only ones? What am I going to do with him when I catch him?*

Matt smiled.

I wonder what Pete would do with him?

It was morning by the time Matt returned to the railroad overpass where he parked the jeep and airplane. Matt slept the clock around. Eventually he opened his eyes but his head didn't want to wake up and he had trouble remembering Seer's movements and contacts. Matt had to tell Bobbie.

A few hours later Matt found the Planter's camp on the side of the road. It was unusual that they were still in camp this time of day. He saw food cooking and water boiling as he entered camp. People were doing the ordinary things that they did everyday.

Young's wagon will be first in line, Matt thought. *The old man doesn't like being in the dust raised by others in front of him.*

Matt was headed toward the Young's wagon when a young man left his fire to meet him. Matt knew him as Mearl and a big frown had replaced the grin that was usually there.

"I'm sure glad you came back today," Mearl said. "I don't know what I should be doin'. I was told to keep away, so I did."

"What were you told to keep away from?"

"I was told to keep away from Grandfather Young's wagons!"

"Did Grandfather Young tell you this?" Matt asked.

"No," Mearl said. "It was Old Mister Diggers from the last wagon."

Matt thought a moment.

"Is that the wagon that the Priest goes in and out of?"

"Yeah," Mearl said. "Diggers took a young wife three summers ago. Couldn't get anything started. No one else could either. Then Father Seer moved in with them and in three months she was sure enough showin' baby."

"Do they always travel in the rear?"

"Since you and Bobbie joined us they have," Mearl

said. "The Preacher has been livin' out in the cactus because he's afraid of you."

"He comes in to get supplies now and then doesn't he?"

"Yeah, I didn't pay any attention but one or two has heard noises out of the Diggers' wagon in the middle of the night. Could be he came for supplies or it could be he came callin' on Diggers' wife. Diggers think the Padre is a saint or a profit and he's here to give us a new savior out of Diggers' woman."

"Where are they now?"

"I don't know. Diggers' wagon is empty, and they told us to stay out of the Young's wagons up ahead there."

"When did Diggers tell you this?"

"It was last evening about bedtime."

Matt felt his stomach tighten as he walked over to the Young's wagon and lifted the back flap. He had to close his eyes and swallow hard. What Matt saw was an act of a beast. Matt ran to the other wagon and he was greeted by a similar scene. The entire Young family was dead, but Bobbie wasn't in either wagon.

Matt counted seventeen people of all ages. How were they kept so quiet while their throats were being cut? Had Diggers and his wife done this? How much did Mearl know?

Matt was demanding.

"Mearl, get over here and look at this."

"I was told to keep away and I was told to keep quiet. I didn't see anything that went on in either wagon, and I didn't hear a sound."

Matt had to threaten Mearl.

"If you don't get over here I'm going to twist off your

head. I want to know how these people were all killed without a sound or a fight."

Mearl's expression never changed as he looked into the back of the first wagon.

"The Diggers were going to say evening prayers with the Young's. Families do that, and they burn some grass while they're in deep thought. Smoke from smolderin' leaves makes you a little more spiritual. Sometimes it takes all night if they burn a lot of leaves, and they burned a lot in here last night. Look at all the ash in the burning bowl. It ain't so much that it makes you helpless when you breath in smoke. Weed smoke helps you to concentrate on one thing, like your prayers."

Matt had to shake Mearl.

"Did Diggers kill all of these people?"

"Diggers wouldn't kill anyone even to protect himself."

"What about his wife?"

"Not her neither."

"Who then?" Matt yelled.

"It was the Padre."

Mearl was hesitant to continue but Matt's face was turning red.

"I have one more question, where is my wife? Where is Bobbie?"

"All I can tell you," Mearl cried out, "is that she never stayed in the wagon when people were having their evening prayers. It was said that she didn't like the smell of the smoke. There are tracks."

Matt followed the tracks for about fifteen minutes before he was able to unravel the events. Four sets of tracks left the wagon not more than twenty minutes ago.

Two sets were small and two were large. The women were ahead of the men and they were running hard. The two larger tracks were irregular and Matt saw signs of stumbling and falling.

Bobbie must have grabbed Mrs. Diggers and ran from the wagon as soon as she realized what was happening inside, Matt thought. *Seer and Diggers figured out that they were gone and they followed behind. The men must be a little groggy and uncoordinated from the smoke. They're stumbling and falling all over the place.*

When Matt stopped and looked back he noticed that Bobbie was curving to the right. She was taking Mrs. Diggers to the back end of camp where Matt usually kept watch.

Matt changed directions and sprinted for the last wagon. He shouted at Mearl as he ran by.

"Bury those people!"

I hope she found a place to hide, Matt thought.

Matt watched Diggers' wagon even though Bobbie's footprints continued across the road into the desert. He was sure that Bobbie was coming to him and he was sure she would do something to let him know where she was.

Matt topped the crest of a hill and found a sharp turn in Bobbie's trail. *She's going back up on the blacktop high way,* Matt thought.

The next time Matt took his eyes off Bobbie's footprints he looked up to find the Priest in the middle of the road lecturing Bobbie and the Diggers man and woman. His message must have been full of venom because he literally snarled the words and he pounded his fists together violently. While looking the other way, father Seer reached in a pocket, raised his hand, and pointed at Matt. To Matt's surprise he fired six shots in his direction.

Before Matt could put his sights on the Father, Seer dropped the gun, pulled a knife from his belt, and swung the blade at Diggers. Diggers grabbed his throat and fell to the ground thus ending Seer's sacrifices. The preacher was executed after he turned and sprinted down the highway.

Padre Seer staggered a few steps his arms outstretched to the side and he toppled over backward into the ditch. Mrs. Diggers stood up, wiped the dust from her dress, and started for the wagons. Mrs. Diggers walked past Bobbie and her dead husband, offering no indication that she understood what had just happened.

Matt and Bobbie buried Father Seer where he fell.

Chapter 24

Pete and Jane spent early spring with Ard and Cleo. It was a quiet time for Pete. Jane had hoped to see an improvement in Pete's breathing, but he continued to cough.

Pete finally took an interest in Stella and Ella. Little-by-little the girls discovered the details of Pete's early years with their father and his mother, and he was full of stories about his grandfather.

The sisters concluded that Pete's hatred of their father was the reason that he was so slow to accept them. The old man and his albino son would always be in the way. Still, misgivings were fading away.

Matt and Bobbie arrived as Pete and Jane were making plans to return to Tinker Shelter and continue on to the Blacktower's family back east.

"Pete," Matt said, "the first thing you need to know is you can forget about Father Seer. I know he bothered you a lot, and he did a lot of damage to people, but we put him in the ground.

Pete nodded his head.

"Good, now you got two days to rest up and be ready

to start east. First stop is the shelter then we be on our way to where you people came from."

Jane, in particular, was very eager to revisit Tinker Shelter.

She wanted to quiz the medical drone and Albedo about helping quiet Pete's cough before it got worse.

The second morning back at Tinker Shelter Pete and Matt started making plans to continue on. Matt expected to drive the steam truck and Pete planned to fly.

"Albedo," Pete said. "We be on our way to see people back where Jane and Matt came from. Jane's medicine teacher wanted me to give this book to you to see if you could explain it.

"Pete," Albedo said. "I will do my best. I hope your trip goes well."

Pete stopped in Chaffee for a quick look.

"The trade center closed its doors," the old bartender said. "The town's about to close up."

By the time the Haze-Blacktower group reached Big Muddy River the heat of mid-day had passed. The flat lands on the other side were cool and wet, and clear skies promised sunny days which heightened the Blacktower's anticipation. Matt unhitched the jeep and trailer and hooked up the trailer to his big steam truck. The smaller vehicle could go faster over the mountains, and Jane would have more time to spend with her sister at the kibbutz. The travelers agreed to meet at Chester Blacktower's last camp.

Pete landed on the highway and taxied to the edge of the road above the temple that was built for Rona Ti and her son. Rona Ti watched as Pete unloaded her things and spoke his parting words to the boy. It was her way to look down when she spoke, but when her words had a stronger meaning she looked directly into Pete's eyes.

"I wish to thank Peter Haze for a place to live, and for saving life, but most of all I wish to thank Peter Haze for a most wonderful son. It would not be possible for me to have more pride in Haze Ti. I will raise him to be a thoughtful leader, but there is no doubt . . . he will be a fighter. When he is old enough he will know our story. If you ever need us . . . we will know and we will come."

Pete rarely smiled but there it was.

"You will be missed," Pete whispered.

Pete followed his map and landed his airplane in the pasture by trucks and trailer houses. It caused great turmoil in the Blacktower yard. Ten minutes later Jane and her kids pulled up in a jeep with a machine gun mounted on top. Matt followed along in the big steam truck.

The Old Man was on his feet and out the door, and a dozen young Blacktowers led the way. He didn't know which way to go first. Jane came at a dead run and jumped into his open arms and she would have bowled him over if Matt hadn't been there to hold him up.

Jane took forever to introduce Pete to her family. As expected, Pete was a little standoffish so Jane added a short story at each introduction. It was something that Jane learned from Rona Ti.

That evening after dinner Jane gathered Daniel's meal and took Pete out to the field where the animals were grazing. She found Daniel sitting on a big boulder watching as she had always done.

"Daniel, come down and meet someone," Jane yelled.

Daniel jumped down by Jane. When he straightened himself he was a full head taller that Jane.

"My goodness, Daniel, you have grown so tall. Pete, this is my next younger brother Daniel, and Daniel, this is my husband, Peter Haze. He likes to be called, Pete."

Pete shook Daniel's hand.

"You got a strong hand, Daniel. That be a good sign."

Daniel was kind of embarrassed.

"You're exactly how I pictured you," Daniel said.

"How be that?"

"I knew you'd be straight and tall and strong like Matt, and you would look like one of the men in the Old Man's book. I had you not much afraid of anything, and you'd have scars and you wouldn't be no run-of-the-mill field hand. I didn't picture you flying an airplane."

"When you be a man and you need an adventure," Pete said, "come to see us. I'll show you the Red Clay Desert. After we be done lookin' Jane will introduce you to a beautiful young woman that be just your age. She will steal your heart away and you'll never be the same."

Jane frowned.

"Cleo and Ard's daughter," Pete said.

"Oh yes, as a matter of fact Ard and Cleo have two daughters so don't come alone," Jane said.

Wildlife remains discovered near two small watering holes had exposed a predicament for Old Man Blacktower. His family had to move and Chester had started making plans before Matt and Jane showed up.

"Bobbie and I decided to return to work with the

family," Matt said. "I think we can still find work where people know us."

The Old Man was pleased to hear about Matt's decision. Chester thought it had been a good life and he had new ideas about things that he and Matt could build.

"After we're quits with this place I would just as soon return to the trek," Chester said. "I can still drive a truck and I can still trade."

Jane smiled. The Old Man was himself again making plans and wanting to take up the trek. He and Matt will make a good team now.

"What are you and Pete going to do?" Daniel asked.

Jane looked at Pete.

"We will be going home to the desert. What about you?"

"I'll go with the trek for two years," Daniel said. "Then I'll be looking for you . . . and that girl."

Jane and Pete were loading the jeep and airplane when Chester called for Pete to come talk to him.

"Pete," the Old Man said. "I had a visitor from up north a while back. He told about a man that might have been from the desert. He asked questions about some people named Chastain. He couldn't remember the traveler's last name."

"I guess he be an older man?"

"I got the impression that he was a little younger than me. My friend said that he was very direct and he was not someone that you wanted trouble with."

"Might be my grandpa. I ain't heard a word about him for several years."

Chapter 25

Pete spent most of his time reading now that he was back home in the shelter. He knew, after the first day, that he needed a direction or goal. Pete had had nothing of interest to occupy his mind. His wife and children were not enough.

I should visit the clan camps, Pete thought. *You never know about those people.*

Pete made the rounds to all the clan camps and found them all uninhabited.

It be time to take Jane and the kids to meet Jones, Pete thought. *Ned and Ted should remember the Haze family.*

A spur-of-the-moment airplane trip such as this was over before Jane knew why they left the shelter. She understood that Pete's Grandpa Kyle went to see Jones for fresh food but that was a long time ago. Pete had been to the Jones farm only twice by himself.

Jones recognized Pete's voice but Pete's face was that of a stranger.

"You gotta be Pete Haze," Jones said. "I guess it's been ten-years that you ain't been here. I see you got one of them air machines to work and you gotta women and kids."

"You ain't wrong," Pete said. "Things change."

"I wouldn't of know'd you without bein' told. I guess the clans is quiet down below. Are they all gone?"

"I be the last one."

Pete's cough had slowly returned and it wasn't long until he was coughing all the time, even in his sleep. Running or exercising made his cough worse and the fumes from the target range stung his lungs.

To keep Pete from pacing up and down the halls in the shelter, Jane suggested that they fly down to see Patch and Ruby.

"Ruby will want to know about her daughters and I wanted to see how the brace was working for James Robert."

Ruby met the airplane on the flat above her tent. She was pleased to see that Jane brought her children, but before they got out of the airplane it was evident that she had something to say.

"Pete, be very careful of Jim Bob. Patch has poisoned up his mind against you and Jim Bob be a big man. He be very strong. Be careful of Patch as well, he's half poisoned his own mind with ideas of who be better and who be best, that, and the Mexican whiskey they bring up from the south. Don't turn your back on either one of them."

"I didn't come here to fight, but I won't back off from one except if you be askin'. I'll answer to you in your home."

Ruby stood a little straighter. She had just been given a compliment and she liked how it felt.

"Now, Jane tell me about my girls."

Patch wasn't so drunk that he didn't recognize Pete.

"Well, it's Pete Haze and family, welcome to my home. Jim Bob say hello to half of your brother, I mean to your half brother."

"Why are you here?" James Robert blurted out.

"Ask Ruby," Pete said, quietly.

Jim Bob got up and walked to a point between Pete and Ruby.

"I don't want the likes of you bothering Ruby. She has work to do."

Jim Bob's comments were punctuated with a loud 'twang', and he pitched forward onto his hands and knees.

Ruby spoke out loud so she would be heard.

"Jim Bob, get out of my way son. These people are going to tell me about my daughters." With that she replaced the iron frying pan on the flagstone hearth.

Ruby spent the hot part of the day mothering Jane's children and asking questions about Stella and Ella. It was a special treat when Jane brought out a loaf of fresh bread and a jar of apple butter. A second jar was fresh ground coffee. A box with cups, plates, and eating utensils had been placed beside the bread.

"These are from the shelter and they belong to Ruby," Jane said.

"It must have been two years ago that we last had real coffee," Ruby said. "Can Jim Bob have some to?"

"It's for everyone," Jane answered.

This was the most peaceful that Jane had ever seen Patch and James Robert. *It must be the food,* She thought. Jim Bob said nothing more the rest of the afternoon.

Patch and Jim Bob were forgotten for nearly three weeks. It was fall and it was cool except for the middle of the day. Pete usually coughed himself awake in the morning. This was followed by several minutes of throat clearing.

In the kitchen, Jane would have something ready to eat, and she expected Pete to be there every morning. After breakfast, roads had to be checked. Old habits die slowly. One morning Pete turned on his cameras and there on the TV screen was the Albino posing for Pete's benefit. Behind Jim Bob, Patch was hovering over a small campfire, and behind Patch two horses and a buggy rested in the shadow of an overpass.

There it be. They came here to put out a challenge, Pete thought. *James Robert must be twenty-one years old, and he wants to make a name for himself and who's going to know. Ain't no one but Patch to show-off for. Jane ain't gonna like it.*

Pete sped the jeep over the highway and down the ramp to the underpass road. He slid to a stop in front of Jim Bob making him give ground. Pete continued pushing his advantage until he had forced the Albino back to his father's fire.

"Patch, how many times do I cut up your little boy? Does he have to die to satisfy you?"

Patch smiled.

"This is all his idea. If he puts you down he thinks that he gets your woman and the shelter."

"In the old days maybe," Pete snarled, "but not any more."

"Jim Bob doesn't know that," Patch said, slurring his

words. "He thinks things are just like they always was. The challenge is still out there."

"And, you expect me to answer a cripple's challenge?" Pete said. "How is he going to fight with the tendons to his hand cut?"

Patch was confident.

"James Robert isn't handicapped. We've trained well beyond the point of compensation for his hand. You aren't trying to weasel out of this are you?"

"You really want this don't you Patch? Okay, only one walks away, in sixty days at the front gate of the old artillery fort. I'll be there at four in the afternoon."

The drunken sneer left Patch's face. He hadn't counted on a fight to the death.

"No guns?" Patch mumbled.

"No guns," Pete repeated.

Jane was pleased that Pete had something to do. He was running his check points by foot both morning and evening, he was working with weights, and he was practicing with his knives the whole middle part of the day. She didn't know what the stimulus was but the glow was back in his eyes, and he was almost happy.

Jane sat on the hilltop with her children watching Pete run out of sight in one direction, and later he would reappear in a different place on the horizon. It was the time of year when the sun felt just as good as the occasional puff of cool air out of the north.

Pete's lungs flared up and Jane asked him to ease up on the training, but he worked harder. For the last half of Pete's training period Jane tried everything that she knew of to treat his problem. He took antibiotics, antihistamines, anti-inflammatory drugs, and vapors. His coughing and throat clearing got better but they continued.

It was time for Pete to tell Jane what he was doing.

"Jane, come talk to me for a minute," Pete said, unexpectedly.

"Are we going somewhere? I saw you working on the jeep."

"I have to go down to the Red River day after tomorrow," Pete answered.

"Why are you going all the way down there?"

"I've been challenged, and only one will walk away."

"I thought the two of you already had this fight," Jane said.

"Patch warped the kids mind," Pete said. "His hand ain't gonna be a hindrance."

"Why don't you tell him that you don't want to fight him?" Jane said.

"It would be a lie," Pete said. "I picked the time and place."

"So you want to fight your half-brother?" Jane asked.

"A challenge be made from him to me."

"Someone is going to die over an insult? Is this another of your male ego events. Why can't you ignore him for Ruby's sake?"

"Ruby understands, you don't."

Pete didn't like to debate over something that had been decided.

"If this is just a fight what's to understand?" Jane's said.

"If I don't answer the challenge, or if he wins and I'm dead, he gets you . . . he don't want the kids."

Jane's mouth fell open.

"This is day-after-tomorrow?"

"Yes," Pete said. "You have to understand that the challenge means we will fight. It'll either be on my terms or it'll be in my house. If I don't finish it once and for all, he will bring the fight up here and involve you in it.

"Don't worry, I ain't afraid of the Albino. I be faster and stronger, and we had the same teacher. I held back last time but not again."

Jane finely understood.

"What about your cough and your lungs?"

"You have my lungs feeling as good as they ever did, and I can hold back the cough if I have to."

"There's no other way?" Jane asked.

Pete shook his head and smiled.

"You can look at it this way, win or lose, my last real fight was over you."

"I asked myself why you were working so hard. You want this fight as much as Patch don't you?"

Pete shrugged his shoulders.

"Jane, whatever happens you keep out of it! Go back and stay with Cleo and Ard if you have to."

Pete landed his airplane on a high way and taxied up to the front gate of the ancient artillery post. No need to go inside there wasn't much left. They could do their fighting right where he was.

The heat of the day was still in the air, the south wind felt good as Pete stretched out in the shade of the airplane wing.

The sound of horses brought Pete to his feet. He had to be ready for anything. Patch and the Albino dismounted. Ruby followed along in a horse drawn buggy but she remained seated.

No one spoke.

Patch started off to one side with the horses, and the Albino made his first lunge at Pete as soon as his horse had stepped out of the way. Jim Bob ended his initial charge with the launching of two knives toward Pete's chest. Pete stepped back and brushed the spinning blades to one side with his own knife.

Pete laughed at Jim Bob.

"Was that Patch's version of a surprise attack? I made ready for that move when I be four-years-old."

Jim Bob turned his back and walked toward Patch. When he next faced Pete he held, in his good hand, a knife that must have been fifteen inches long, and there wedged in place over his withered hand and wrist he wore a metal cover firmly bound in place.

Pete understood why Patch said there would be no disadvantage due to the injured hand. The metal cover had two six-inch blades attached and the metal cover could be used as a shield. He could charge in behind the shield, and he wouldn't have to retreat from a cutting blow to the arm.

Patch was seated on a half-buried boulder and a big smile lit up his face. The smile left Patch's face as Pete brought a second knife into view. The second knife was fitted with brass knuckles which provided considerable protection for his hand. Patch immediately encouraged James Robert to end the fight.

"Be quick about ending this and you can drive the jeep home. I don't want to sit around here all night."

For the first hour the Albino tried to take advantage of his longer knife. His intent was to hold Pete back with his shield and cut at his arm with his longer blade. All that he managed were a few scratches.

Pete knew after the first hour that he was going to outlast the Albino. The White One was sweating and wheezing as he jumped back from Pete's every low-level charge and slash attack. When he needed to catch his breath Jim Bob held the knife at arms length in front as he gasped for air. Pete, with all his strength, brought his heavy steel blade down on the blade that was pointed at him. The Albino's long knife flew from his hand making him vulnerable.

Jim Bob had to ward off the next two attacks with his shield. The third swing of Pete's knife was a false attack intended to keep the shield held high. Pete rolled in low and stuck his second knife deep into the Albino's thigh. Jim Bob was cut to the bone and blood went everywhere.

Jim Bob managed to pull his third knife as he fell backward. He stabbed and kicked wildly when Pete rolled on through his low angle attack.

Pete saw that Jim Bob didn't press the attack when Pete rolled under his protected arm. It was difficult for Jim Bob to keep his balance, and he dragged his left leg when he moved to the right, and he staggered some when he was forced to the left.

Pete's next attack put four deep cuts on the Albino, he could no longer protect himself, and Pete gave him less than ten minutes.

Ruby stood in the carriage. Her head was hanging as though she was the one being defeated.

Jim Bob was wild eyed and he was looking left and right. He expected help. He fell time after time and Pete was on him but the shield forced Pete back. The Albino was up and trying to run but his legs would not allow him to escape. Jim Bob was being cut to shreds, and Patch was livid.

Patch, venting his anger, screamed orders and he berated Jim Bob. The next time Jim Bob fell he reached inside his bloody shirt, pulled a small revolver, and shot Pete in the chest.

Slowly Jim Bob got to his feet turning to look at Patch.

Patch, for once, was speechless. Jim Bob raised the revolver and shot him three times.

This wasn't how Pete said it would go. Pete's rule said no guns. Jim Bob shot him at point blank range.

A fifth shot forced the Albino to stagger backward holding his neck. A sixth shot rang out and the white one fell to the ground on top of Pete.

Ruby pushed the carbine back into the scabbard, and she led her horse and carriage over to the people on the ground. She checked each one of the men before she gathered wood and started a fire. When the fire was burning well Ruby started digging with tools that were taken from the carriage. She came prepared to bury someone.

Jane wrapped her children in army blankets and pulled them close to her before she took the wheel of the jeep. She had Pete's map to follow. Jane struggled to keep her voice from quivering when she talked.

"Children, listen to me. We have to deal with some bad news. Your father is fighting with Jim Bob and they may have killed each other. We're going down to the fight and see what happened."

The next morning Jane found Ruby's fire and she decided to pull off the road to see what Ruby was doing. With the help of binoculars, Jane saw what appeared to be two graves, and Ruby was working on something in her carriage. In due course the fire died and Ruby left.

The children stood in the back seat as Jane started the jeep and drove down to the front gate of the old army post.

"Kids stay in the jeep and be quiet. I need to figure out what happened here."

Jane had no digging tools in the jeep. She had to pull clods of clay out of the grave by hand. It was a slow process. The grave was deeper than she thought it would be. Her hands were bruised and bleeding by the time she reached the head. She pulled the shroud away from the face and recoiled at the sight. The ghostly appearance of James Robert was a shock but it gave her a little hope. He was so white and she saw bullet holes in his neck and head.

Jane promptly kicked clumps of clay back in the Albino's face. She turned and started scratching at the mound of clay over the other grave. By the time she found the body Jane's hands could take no more abuse. Unfortunately for Jane, the body had been placed other-way-around and she had unwittingly uncovered a pair of boots.

The boots that Jane found came from the shelter and no one else had boots like Pete's. Pete was in the grave beside Jim Bob. *They would never be satisfied until one or both of them were dead,* Jane thought. Jane wanted to see Pete's face but she had to find cover for her children. Midday heat was forcing her to move on.

An old brick school building south of the fort gave her all the protection she needed for the children and the jeep. Jane sat on the floor and leaned back against the wall. Her hands were so sore that she couldn't make a fist.

Jane thought about the boots and she realized that they were the last thing of Pete's that she was going to see.

Jane didn't want to return to the shelter . . . not without Pete, she didn't even want to stop. Jane was forced by circumstance pick up things that she needed for travel.

Jane thought about going home to her family but Cleo and Ard were closer and Jane needed someone to lean on.

Ruby's predicted the result of Jim Bob's training shortly after Patch installed himself as James Robert's trainer and philosophy guide. She knew then, that one day it would be up to her to put an end to it. Ruby shed no tears for the boy she had been forced to suppress her emotions more than thirty-years ago.

The bonfire had almost burned itself out by the time Ruby was satisfied with the depth of her effort. She pulled the boy into the grave and covered him with his blanket. Ruby mumbled her prayer for the dead as she dropped a handful of dirt on the blanket. She started Pete's grave next to Jim Bob's and she shoveled from one grave into the other.

When Jim Bob's grave was full of clay Ruby climbed

out and pulled Pete into his resting place. She scooped up a handful of loose soil and dropped it on Pete and mumbled the same prayer. As she turned her back and filled her shovel she heard a coughing spasm from the grave.

On hands and knees Ruby peered over the edge of the grave and she witnessed Pete opening his eyes. She saw him grimace in pain as he fought back another coughing fit. Ruby looked at Patch, "Pete is still alive, Jim Bob didn't kill him!" But Patch couldn't hear, he was dead. Pete was spitting up blood as Ruby turned away from the grave.

Ruby parked the carriage by the grave and she used a rope, a plank, and a horse to lift Pete into the carriage. She soaked a clean rag with her drinking water and washed Pete's face and cleaned his wound. With strips of material from an old blanket Ruby tightly wrapped his chest in an effort to reduce movement in his rib cage.

Patch was hastily pulled into the grave and covered with clumps of clay. Ruby mumbled the prayer as she piled on the last clod.

Ruby had to tie Pete to the carriage seat to keep him from falling out. If the trip didn't kill him, he had a chance because she had considerable experience treating gunshot wounds.

Ruby kept the horses running because she had four to interchange, and going slow wasn't going to reduce the amount of blood that Pete lost. The bullet was going to keep the wound open and bleeding. It had to come out as quickly as possible and her bullet extractors were back at her camp.

Ruby's tent was in sight by midmorning. Pete was still

breathing the last time she stopped to change horses, but now, as the carriage rolled on, she couldn't tell. Maybe it was best if he was unconscious until the trip was over and the bullet was out, and maybe it was best if he couldn't feel the tickle in his throat that would start him coughing again.

During the days and nights that followed Ruby wasn't always sure that Pete was recovering. The bullet was small and it had involved his lung but the entry had missed bone.

Most of the time Pete appeared to be unconscious, but he didn't cough and that was a good sign. He didn't run much of a temperature either. She didn't understand it but she took it as another good sign.

She knew that Pete would have no interest in food but she tried everyday to give him spoonfuls of water with a few grains of sugar and salt in it. And, she had him breathing herbal vapors in steam. She had faith that the vapors would help heal his lung. She had seen it work before.

It had been two weeks and the only change in his condition was in the amount of fluid draining from his chest when the wrap was removed and cleaned. It was a little less each day and the color changed from red to amber. Ruby breathed a sigh of relief when Pete asked for water and he was able to stand.

Pete's convalescence was painfully slow. It was a month-and-a-half before Ruby could remove the wrap and let the wound in his chest to heal shut.

Pete discovered that he could walk without irritating his lung. Slowly his walks got longer and longer until he

JOE ALLEN

was walking all night. He felt strength returning to his legs.

Pete stopped spitting up blood, but best of all, tightness in his chest and shortness of breath were gone. For the first time since he was taken into Ruby's tent he felt completely recovered and strong. He knew that his muscles had withered a great deal, so it wasn't physical strength that he felt. It was the psychological strength of knowing that once more he was in charge.

Pete wanted to build up his endurance before he returned to Jane and his children. He pushed himself hard and his lung held, and he talked a little about going home again.

Ruby was pleased that she was able to keep Pete alive but she couldn't tell where her efforts ended and his will power began. Pete's determination had earned Ruby's respect and she couldn't help but compare him with her son. There were so few similarities considering they had the same father.

As with many desert people Ruby and Pete didn't need words at first. Pete had understood that he was about to bleed to death and he knew that he could not allow himself even one more coughing spasm.

Over the weeks Ruby saw to his every need without being asked. She waited and watched for the bleeding to stop and she knew when the tickle in his throat was gone. She knew when to help him up and she knew when to stand back. She knew when he needed solid food and she knew when he needed sleep. She knew that he was grateful for her help and she knew that someday he would ask her to come live in the shelter.

Eventually, Pete's strength returned. During his

recovery he had learned what it was like to be vulnerable and his arrogance was tempered somewhat by this feeling, but his confidence returned with the return of his abilities. He could run for hours without fatigue and he trained without limitations.

Physically, Pete had never felt better. The time had come to return to the shelter. Inside, he sat on his heels looking into the fire while Ruby stirred something for their meal.

"When you're ready, I want you to come live at the Tinker Shelter with us," Pete said.

"I know," Ruby answered.

"How be you about flying?" Pete asked.

"I'm okay," Ruby answered.

Pete sat quietly for several minutes before speaking.

"Tomorrow we go see to the airplane. If it be working good we leave from there. Be ready."

Ruby nodded her head absentmindedly.

Pete's plans were sketchy, but he thought that he should take Ruby with him to Tinker Shelter and give her a chance to get acquainted with his place. While she looked around he could do maintenance on his airplane.

After landing Pete and Ruby found the shelter empty.

"Jane must think I be dead. She probably took the kids and went to live with her people. I be gettin' the airplane ready to go lookin'. What do you want to do while I'm gone?"

Ruby didn't want to live alone.

"Pete, I think I would like to go see my girls. Would

it be out-of-your-way to take me there before you left to find Jane?"

"It ain't a problem," Pete said. "Why didn't I think? You got grandchildren."

Pete buzzed Ard and Cleo's ranch house once to let them know that they were about to have company. Several people came out shielding their eyes from the sun. Pete landed his airplane and taxied into position where he had parked his machine. Ruby got out and walked around the wing toward the house. Pete got out and kneeled under the wings to put anchors in the ground.

Cleo and several of her family were walking out to greet their visitors when one of Cleo's boys yells, "It's Pete!"

Jane had been standing in the door when she recognized Pete. She dropped to her knees holding her hands over her mouth unable to react to the sight in front of her. Then with the power of rekindled passion Jane bolted out the door scattering those in her way.

Chapter 26

Six months back in the shelter Pete needed something to occupy his mind. It occurred to him that Chester Blacktower mentioned his Grandfather. Pete had often reminisced about the return of his grandpa Kyle, consequently it didn't take long for Pete to make a decision.

"I be goin' to find my granddad and bring him back to live with us if he be willing."

"When are you leaving?" Jane asked.

"Tomorrow," Pete answered.

Message to Pete from Albedo:

Concerning the 'book' that you asked me to evaluate:

The item is a disguised communication device.

It is not a library book. The numbers on the back have nothing to do with a standard library placement code. The interior of the tome has meaningless printed pages in the front half and back half. Between the two halves I found four pages like nothing I have ever witnessed. I believe that this special section works with a photo-recorder/transmitter to transfer pictographs to a receiver.

Twenty-four pictographs are visible. Although 16th Century Spanish missionaries destroyed much from this era, Pre-Columbian codices from Mesoamerica and South America helped form an opinion. I am able to suggest the following as part of the last transmission:

1. The atmosphere is excessively corruptive.
2. Disease organisms thrive.
3. Two items of value: Green plants & saltwater
4. Attempted colonization is not doing well.

A repeat attempt is not suggested.